ALADDIN RELIGHTED

THE ALADDIN TRILOGY #1

ALADDIN RELIGHTED

THE ALADDIN TRILOGY #1

J.R. RAIN
PIERS ANTHONY

ACCLAIM FOR J.R. RAIN AND PIERS ANTHONY:

"Anthony's most ambitious project to date. Well conceived and written from the heart."
—**Library Journal** on Piers Anthony's *Isle of Woman*

"Be prepared to lose sleep!"
—**James Rollins**, international bestselling author of *The Doomsday Key*

"Piers Anthony is a writer of passion. *Volk* is a masterpiece."
—**Brad Linaweaver**, author of *Moon of Ice*

"*Dark Horse* is the best book I've read in a long time!"
—**Gemma Halliday**, award-winning author of *Spying in High Heels*

"Piers Anthony is one of the more colorful personalities in the SF world."
—***Science Fiction Chronicle*** on Piers Anthony's *Bio of an Ogre*

"*Moon Dance* is a must read. If you like Janet Evanovich's Stephanie Plum, bounty hunter, be prepared to love J.R. Rain's Samantha Moon, vampire private investigator."
—**Eve Paludan**, author of *Letters from David*

OTHER BOOKS BY PIERS ANTHONY AND J.R. RAIN

STANDALONE NOVELS

Dragon Assassin

Dolfin Tayle

Jack and the Giants

THE ALADDIN TRILOGY

Aladdin Relighted

Aladdin Sins Bad

Aladdin and the Flying Dutchman

Aladdin Relighted

License Notes

ISBN: 1500676292
ISBN 13: 9781500676292

ACKNOWLEDGMENT

A special thank you to Sandy.

ALADDIN RELIGHTED AUTHORS' PREFACE

The Arabian Nights tales, supposedly told over the course of one thousand and one nights, constitute a huge and wonderful fantasy collection. Their framework is that a king, enraged by the infidelity of his wife, set up a policy of marrying a woman, spending a single night with her, then executing her in the morning so she would have no chance to be unfaithful. Thus a woman a night, indefinitely. But after a while there was coming to be a shortage of eligible maidens in the kingdom. Something had to be done. But who dared caution the king about his policy?

Finally the vizier's daughter Shahrazad or Scheherazade, a lovely and savvy girl, volunteered to marry the king. She had a plan. She had her younger sister accompany her to the bridal suite, and after the king had fulfilled his conjugal duty, the sister begged Shahrazad to tell her a story. The king happened to be restless, so was amenable; stories are great entertainments the world over.

Shahrazad began her story, full of magic and wonder, but before she finished it the night was over and it was time to commence the day. In the story a demon was raising his sword to kill a merchant. The king was overcome by curiosity to know how that came out. So he spared Shahrazad for another night, so that she could tell the rest before she died. But she did not finish the story the second night, so the king granted another continuance. So it continued for almost three years, and Shahrazad had birthed more than one baby. The king finally realized that she was a fully worthy and faithful wife, and elected not to execute her. Thus the decimation of maidens was halted, and the kingdom prospered.

This was of course a convenient framework for the vast collection of Arabian folklore. Piers Anthony adapted one of those stories, *Hasan*, as a novel over 40 years ago, but there are many more. Thus "The Story of Aladdin and the Magic Lamp." In that one a boy manages to acquire both a magic ring and a magic lamp, and the powers this gave him enabled him to win the king's daughter and in due course inherit the throne itself.

One problem. It's a fake. "Aladdin" was not one of the original tales. Shahrazad never told it to the king. It was written in Paris in the eighteenth century, translated to Arabic, and, taken for a legitimate tale, translated to English.

Thus the present story, *Aladdin Relighted*, is a kind of sequel to a fake. Purists may wonder why the characters are not shown bowing toward Mecca five times a day or honoring other Muslim conventions other than token references. Well, the original story was set in China, where Muslim conventions do not prevail and djinni do not circulate; that is perhaps another signal of its fakery. So we felt free to do it our own way. It is fantasy adventure with an Arabian Night's flavor. We use the terms djinn, jinn, genie and ifrit interchangeably, though in Arabic lore there are sophisticated distinctions. We thought it would be fun to do the tale, relating to Aladdin's later life, and it was. We trust that most readers will enjoy it as the light-hearted effort it is, and that Shahrazad herself would have found it worthy. We don't want anyone executing *us* the morning after.

CHAPTER ONE

The Middle-East,
A Forgotten Desert

She was a fine beauty with almond-shaped eyes, high cheekbones and lips so full they could hardly close. She stepped into my tent and shook out her hair and slapped the trail dust from her overcoat.

I had been dozing lightly, one foot propped up on a heavy travel chest, when I heard a woman's voice asking for me. With my foot still hanging over the ornately-engraved chest, I had turned my head with some interest and watched as a dark-haired woman had poked her head in my open tent. My tent was always open. After all, I was always open for business. Once confirming she had the right tent, she had strode in confidently.

And that's when I sat up, blinking hard. It was not often that such a beauty entered my humble tent. Granted, there had been a time when I was surrounded by such beauties, but that seemed like a long, long time ago.

"Do you always sleep during the day?" she asked. As she spoke, she scanned my simple tent, wrinkling her nose. She stepped over to a low table and looked down at a carving of mine. She nodded to herself, as if she approved of my handiwork. She looked around my tent some more, and when she was done, she looked at me directly, perhaps challengingly.

"Only until the sun goes down."

She had been looking at a pile of my dirty robes sitting in one corner of my tent. She snapped her head around. "I hope you're joking."

"And why would you hope that?"

"Because I will not hire a sluggard."

She was a woman of considerable wealth, that much was for sure. She also did not act like any woman I had even seen, outside of the many courtyards and palaces I had once been accustomed to. She reminded me of all that was wrong with wealth and royalty and I immediately took a disliking to her, despite her great beauty.

Through my tent opening came the sounds of money being exchanged for any number of items. At the opening, swirling dust still hovered in the air from when she had entered. The dust caught some of the harsh sunlight, forming phantasmagorical shapes that looked vaguely familiar.

"And why would my lady need to hire a lazy wretch like me?" I asked. As I spoke I lifted my sandled foot off the chest and sat back with my elbows on my knees.

"Emir Farid said some satisfactory things about you. In particular, that you have proven to be somewhat reliable."

"Emir Farid has always greatly admired me."

She studied me closely. Her almond-shaped eyes didn't miss much. Her long fingers, I saw, were heavy with jewels.

"Aren't you going to offer me a seat?" she asked.

I motioned to the area in front of the chest. The area was covered in sand and didn't look much different than the desert outside my tent.

I really ought to clean this place, I thought.

"Never mind," she said. "I'll stand."

I shrugged and grinned. She fanned her face and looked around my tent some more. She didn't seem pleased, but she also looked desperate. Desperate usually won out.

She said, "Despite your many flaws, according to Emir Farid, he says that you are particularly adept at...finding things."

"I'm also adept at losing things, my lady, but funny how no one seems to want to hire me for that."

Outside, a few tents down, an animal shrieked, followed by sounds of splashing, and I knew a goat had been slaughtered. A dry, hot wind found its way into my tent, swirling the dirt at her feet, and lifting her robe around her ankles.

Nice ankles.

She caught me looking at them and leveled a withering stare at me. I grinned some more.

"You make a lot of jokes," she said. "This could be a problem."

I moved to sit back in the position she had found me in. "Then I wish you luck in your quest to find whatever it is that's missing. May I suggest you take a look around our grand market place. Perhaps this thing of which you seek is under your very nose." I closed my eyes and folded my hands over my chest.

"Are you always like this?" she demanded.

"Lying down? Often."

She made a small, frustrated noise. "Is there anyone else in this godforsaken outpost who can help me?"

"There's a shepherd who's been known to be fairly adept at finding lost goats—although, come to think of it, he did lose one last week—"

"Enough," she snapped. "I don't have much time and you will have to do, although you are older than I had hoped."

"My lady is full of compliments. I am not sure if I should blush or sleep."

"Neither, old man. Come, there's much to do."

I heard her step towards the open flap of my tent. I still hadn't opened my eyes. I lifted my hand and rested it on the corner of the chest. I hunkered deeper on the padding that doubled as my bed. She stopped at the entrance.

"Well?" she asked impatiently.

"Well what?"

"Aren't you coming?"

I turned my head and looked at her. She was standing with her hands on her hips, silhouetted in the streaming sunlight. God, she was beautiful. And irritating.

I said, "Not until I know what you want me for and we have discussed my price."

She turned and faced the bustling marketplace just outside my tent. She wanted to leave. She wanted to run. But she needed my help, that much was obvious. I waited, smiling contentedly to myself.

She said, "If I tell you on the trail, I will double your asking price."

Double was good. I jumped to my feet and grabbed a satchel and my chest. The rest could stay.

At the tent entrance, I nodded at her. "You have yourself a deal."

CHAPTER TWO

I followed her out, blinking in the bright sunlight. Even my brief pause put her ahead of me, as she was already moving purposefully down the street. I refused to be seen scrambling after her like a hungry mongrel, so I lengthened my stride and slowly caught up.

"Some details remain," I said as I drew within range.

"They can wait."

"Such as my fee. I want half in advance."

She didn't hesitate. She simply flipped something at me. I caught it. It was a gold piece. That would do.

"Such as your name."

"I am Enees-el-Jenees, of a prominent family, but I prefer to be incognito for now."

"I will abbreviate it to Jewel," I agreed. "And I of course am Niddala, as you surely know." It was my name spelled backwards. No one seemed to have caught on, which probably indicated disinterest rather than stupidity. I had fallen far since my heyday.

"Niddala the Thief," she agreed.

"Niddala the specialist in locating hidden objects."

"Have it your way."

"Now tell me the nature of the mission. What, precisely, am I expected to find?"

"My young son."

This set me back. "Normally mothers know the whereabouts of their offspring."

"He was stolen from me. It's a devious story."

"Have it your way," I agreed.

She shot me a wrathful glance. "I will tell it when we are more private." She approached a small parked carriage. It was closed, with a buckboard for the driver, and two fine horses were hitched to it. "Get in."

"This is an intercity transport," I protested. "Where are we going?"

"I hired it for the occasion. Get in."

"Where are we going?" I repeated, putting my two feet down with audible impacts, signaling my refusal to go further on faith.

"Samarkand." She stepped impatiently to the coach herself, evidently tired of my dawdling.

Oh, camel dung! I hated that city, and not just because of its reputation for killing innocent travelers. But it would not be expedient to go into that with her at the moment. "You didn't say we were going so far away."

"You didn't ask. Now help me in, making a pretense of masculinity, and join me inside. Time is brief."

I made an interior sigh and put a firm hand to her elbow to steady her as she took the steep step up. Her ascent showed one ankle right up to the calf, putting me in mind of certain luscious slave girls I had known in my better days. But did I really want to do this?

I paused outside. I rubbed my brass ring in a certain way. Immediately there was an invisible presence beside me. "I am here, master." This was El Fadl, the ifrit of the ring, not one of the top tier of the djinn, but a serviceable aide and companion. He was especially useful when a target object was highly guarded. In fact I owed much of my reputation as a location specialist—okay, thief—to his dexterous supernatural touch.

"Faddy," I murmured. "She wants me to go to Samarkand."

"Samarkand! Don't you know better, master? Give her back her gold piece."

"I need the money. But you had better do due diligence on her, and let me know soon, just in case I do need to give it back."

"I hear and obey, Nid," he agreed, and faded.

"Well?" Jewel called imperiously from within.

"On my way," I called back, and climbed reluctantly into the coach.

It was tight within, with barely room for two facing each other if our knees interspliced. Actually that aspect was interesting; her knees felt firm and smooth. Who knew what divine flesh they attached to? I had barely gotten seated when the coach jerked into motion. We were on our way.

"This is the situation," Jewel said briskly. "I was wrongly accused of conspiracy by my wicked ex-husband, and imprisoned for two years until I was released."

"Released?" I asked dubiously.

"I finally seduced my captors and killed them when they were distracted. I recovered some of my assets my husband hadn't known about, rendering them into these rings, as only what is on my person is safe. Now I am anonymous, but mean to recover my innocent son. I will do what it takes to accomplish my purpose."

Hence her interest in hiring a nonentity. Had she gone about her mission openly, her husband's spies would have been alerted, and killed her, or at least imprisoned her again.

"You seduced and killed them," I repeated.

"A man isn't expecting a knife in the gut when he is in the throes of fulfillment. That is when he is most vulnerable."

"Is that a warning to me not to get ideas?"

"No. Your reputation is for thieving, not raping. If you have a problem about going to Samarkand, would a seduction alleviate it?"

"It might," I agreed.

"You were supposed to angrily deny it!"

"I am a thief and a liar," I said seriously. "But I do not steal from or lie to those who hire me. You have bought my loyalty for the mission. But I do have reason to avoid Samarkand, and your favors might indeed mitigate my aversion. I am not demanding them, merely answering your question."

She gazed intently at me a moment. "You may be more of a man than I took you for."

"And you may be more of a woman."

She was silent, perhaps digesting that.

"Master," Fadl's voice came in my ear.

I cocked my head slightly, indicating that I was listening.

"The woman is being shadowed by armed men. She is not as anonymous as she may choose to believe. My guess is that if she goes to Samarkand, she will be killed. There are horsemen lurking nearby, maybe awaiting their chance to catch the coach out of sight of the authorities. You have only a few minutes to avoid them."

I nodded. "Slow the carriage," I murmured.

"I hear and obey." Fadl faded.

"What did you say?" Jewel asked.

"I was muttering," I said. "Jewel, you are in danger. We must get out of this coach in a hurry."

"I paid a valuable jewel for this ride!" she protested. "I am *not* going to walk to Samarkand!"

"Trust me."

She stared at me, obviously not trusting me.

The coach swerved and slowed as Fadl made his distraction, perhaps spooking the horses with a ghostly smell.

"What is happening?" Jewel asked, alarmed.

I leaned forward and grabbed the driver's shoulder. He looked back, startled. He was an older Arab, with sharp eyes.

"There's danger ahead, friend. We must abandon this carriage."

His eyes narrowed, but before he could answer, Jewel screeched behind me, "What the devil are you talking about?"

I ignored her. "Come," I said to him, "we don't have much time!"

He shook his head. "I see no danger—"

Faddy whispered in my ear, "Go now!"

The carriage had slowed enough. I tossed my special lockbox out the side of the wagon. It landed in the sand and rolled. Next, I grabbed Jewel's arm. "Jump out with me. *Now!*" I plunged out, hauling her along with me.

We landed and rolled in the sand. At another time I would really have noticed the way her soft body jammed against mine, but at the moment I was trying to see that she suffered no injury.

The driver got control of the horses, who seemed no longer distracted, and the coach accelerated. The driver looked back, no doubt wondering where his passengers had disappeared to.

"Of all the ridiculous stunts!" she expostulated as we got back on our feet. She remained beautiful even when disheveled, maybe even more so, as more of her body showed. "You didn't need to do this to get me alone! We were alone in the coach."

"Get under cover," I said tersely, hauling her to a nearby copse. "And be silent."

She obeyed with ill grace. We settled in the copse, looking out at the coach that was now leaving us well behind.

Nearby, I saw my valuable travel chest, resting in some scraggly brush. For now, I let it be.

Four horsemen converged on the vehicle. In moments they cut the coachman down and left him bleeding in the sand. Then they ripped open the coach doorway. Even from the distance their curses were audible as they discovered it was empty.

"*Now* I trust you," Jewel said.

CHAPTER THREE

"What do we do?" asked Jewel.

I brought my fingers to my lips, shushing her. The soldiers were examining the coach carefully. They ignored the bleeding driver, heedless of his misery. Thus far, we had not been spotted, but it would only be a matter of time. After all, there was a nice deep trail leading through the sand and directly towards us. The copse itself was small and offered little opportunity for concealment.

One of the men shouted at the moaning driver, no doubt demanding to know where we had gone. The driver, to his credit, appeared not to answer, although it was hard to tell from this distance. Or perhaps he was dead. The guard shouted again and drew his sword. He pointed it down at the driver's neck.

"You there, Faddy?" I asked, subvocalizing my words.

"Always, master."

"You can quit calling me master."

"Do you really want to get into this now, master?"

"No," I said. "Cause a distraction. Quick. I do not want to see this driver perish."

"But the driver did not heed your warning."

"Just do it."

"As you wish," said Faddy, followed a moment later by a barley audible, "Master."

"Did you say something?" asked Jewel.

"No," I said. "Did you?"

"No, but I thought I heard something—never mind. They're going to kill Jabeer. I can't look."

"Hurry!" I whispered to Faddy.

As the guard raised his curved scimitar, its polished steel catching some of the intense afternoon sun, there came a loud shout from the distant mountains. The shout, amazingly, sounded much like me. Faddy never ceased to amaze. Another shout followed, one that sounded much like Jewel. Both voices echoed over the desert.

One of the soldiers pointed, and immediately the driver was forgotten. In haste, the soldiers mounted their horses, and turned toward the distant voices. They disappeared a moment later, kicking up a billowing cloud of dust as they cut through the desert and far away from us.

Jewel was staring at me. She had heard the voices, too, of course. My voice and her own voice.

"What the devil is going on?" she asked.

"I'll explain later," I said, reaching down for her hand. She took mine and I hauled her to her feet. Perhaps a little too roughly. She stumbled forward and into me. I held her briefly, my hand at the small of her back. I gave her a lopsided grin. "Come," I said. "Your driver needs our help."

I retrieved my wooden lockbox—which had survived the tumble unscathed, as I knew it would—and we made our way back up the sandy slope and to the road.

Without shade, the sun was merciless. Heatwaves rose up from the hard-packed road, and I had long ago broken out in a pouring sweat, which soaked through my tunic. I glanced over at Jewel. There might have been a slight gleam of sweat on her upper lip.

In the far distance, I could mark the soldier's path from the rising dust plumes. They were much too far away to see us. And besides, every now and then, I could hear Faddy leading them further and further away. Allah bless Faddy.

As we approached the coach, I could hear the driver's faint moans, which seemed to agitate the two powerful, Arabian horses. I picked up my pace and was soon by the driver's side. I set aside my chest and examined the man's wounds. Not good. My best guess was that he would die within a day. But he would not die alone in this heat.

As I examined him, his dazed eyes searched my face. He opened his mouth to speak and blood spilled out. "How…how did you know?" he asked.

"Don't talk now, old man. You're going to need your strength."

"I should have—"

I winked at him. "Shush, and yes you should have."

I tore off a long stretch of his dust-covered robe and did my best to dress his wound. Blood quickly soaked through the bandage, but it would have to do.

"You seem to have all the answers," Jewel said to me, as she knelt down to examine the wounded man. As she did so, she laid her hand tenderly on his tear-streaked cheek, and he responded with a weak smile. "You will be fine, Jabeer," she said to him.

He actually laughed, and as he did, more blood dribbled out of the corner of his mouth. "You are a fine liar, my lady."

She looked at me sharply, her almond-shaped eyes dark and challenging, and about as beautiful as anything I had ever seen. That thought, of course, pulled at my heartstrings, and I immediately felt guilty. "So what do we do now, Mr. Answer Man?" she asked.

I did not need Faddy to tell me the main road to Samarkand was unsafe. Her ex-husband, whoever he was, was surely a powerful man with many available resources. As we stood there in the hot sun, as the horses whinnied and pawed at the ground, and as a man lay dying at my feet, I knew what we had to do, and I didn't like it.

"We need to get off the main road. The soldiers will be back, especially once they realize they have been duped."

"Duped? What the devil are you talking about? Wait, let me guess. You'll explain later."

I winked. "Now you're catching on," I said.

I unhitched the horses and spent some time securing what little valuables we had; or, rather, securing what little valuables we absolutely needed. Jewel protested over the exclusion of most of her wardrobe and accessories, but I ignored her protests, which seemed to infuriate her. Jabeer himself was absolutely adamant that his own small satchel be included, which included an elaborate bedroll. I was about to ignore him, too, but he became so insistent that I grudgingly acquiesced and found a spot for his belongings.

Once I had the horses ready for travel, Jewel and I carefully heaved the wounded man onto a horse. Once on, I leaped up behind him and held him in place. If the added wight bothered the great Arabian horse, he did not show it. Jewel followed suit on her own mount, and I led the way back down the steep sandy slope.

"Where are we going?" Jewel called out to me.

"There's another way," I said, "one that will lead us to Samarkand."

Jabeer actually turned his head and looked back at me, fear in his dark eyes. "No," he whispered.

He, of course, would have known of the road, which, for all intents and purposes, wasn't much of a road at all. It was an ancient trail that led through the heart of what some claim were enchanted mountains. Enchanted, or cursed, depending on who you spoke with. Still, most people were in agreement of one thing: Only the most foolish ventured upon it. And those who did were seldom seen alive again. That is, of course, if you believed in such fantastical tales.

I didn't. Besides, I had a few tricks up my own sleeve.

I patted Jabeer lightly on his stooped shoulder. "Don't look so nervous, old man."

"Please, this isn't wise."

"I would have to agree, master," said Faddy in my ear.

"Is there another way?" I sub-vocalized.

The djinn paused before answering. "As of now, no."

"Rest now, my friend. I may need you later."

"Of that, I have no doubt, master."

"And quit calling me master."

"Yes, master."

At the bottom of the slope, I turned my mount to the east, toward a great chain of shimmering mountains, and as as we cut across the sun-baked earth, two vultures slowly circled above.

I did my best to ignore them.

CHAPTER FOUR

The pace was slow, because the horses were overloaded and not trained for riding; they were carriage haulers. I knew that our chances of reaching the mountains before the raiders caught up to us were next to nil.

Jewel knew it too. "Those ruffians won't be distracted long. Then they'll orient on our trail and catch us within the hour."

"They will," I agreed grimly.

"You have planned for this contingency?"

"Naturally," I agreed, cudgeling my balky mind for some viable plan. I knew the raiders would not be fooled by spot diversions again.

"Why is Jabeer so alarmed?"

"Must be delirium from the fever of his wounds."

Jabeer, not completely out of it, made a weak chuckle. He knew he would soon be dead regardless, so he could be halfway objective. He was concerned about the risk to Jewel, not himself.

"It's a good thing I have confidence in you, Niddala," she said ironically.

I touched my ring. Faddy responded immediately, as was his wont. "Master."

"Is there any cover we can reach within the hour?"

"Just a dried up oasis. No food or water there, just rocks and bones. Some think it's haunted."

"Is it?"

"Yes."

"Good. Where?"

“East south east from here.”

“Thanks, Faddy. Begone.”

“Master, those haunts are weak. They won’t stop the raiders.”

“Are you getting deaf in your senility? I said Begone.”

“…and obey, master,” he said disapprovingly, and was gone.

“You have a djinn!” Jabeer said.

“Just a no-account ifrit, bottom tier. He can’t do much except spy and some illusion. But I like him.”

“He can’t stop the raiders.”

“He can’t stop the raiders,” I agreed. “But I have tricks of my own. Now stop wasting your energy talking to me.”

“I’m done for anyway.”

“Probably,” I agreed. “But if we make the mountains, there may be healing elixir.”

“Along with dragons, curses, and worse.”

I shrugged. “One has to take the ill with the good.”

“You’re an utter fool,” he said admiringly. “No wonder Jewel likes you.”

“She’d as soon gut me as kiss me.”

“True. But most men in her mind rate only the gutting. Still, don’t push your luck.”

“I’m hired help. I have no ideas about her.”

“And you’re a liar too. If you’re a man, you have ideas about her.”

“Oh? You too?”

“I served as her hired driver before her ass of a husband dumped her and framed her. She never noticed me, but I used to dream what it would be like with her in bed before she threatened to gut me. Might have been worth it.”

“Might be,” I agreed.

He sank into troubled slumber. It had been an interesting dialogue.

We reached the oasis. It was exactly as Faddy had described. Dead trees, deserted stone huts, a low spot where there had once been a spring, and bones.

“Rest yourself,” I told Jewel. “We’re bound to have company soon.” I dismounted and helped Jabeer half-fall off. I got him settled in the shade of a tumbled wall.

"I'll tend to Jabeer," she said.

"Be kind to him. He's not long for the mortal realm."

"I know." She took the man's hand and kissed it. "You have been a good and faithful servant," she told him.

Jabeer was dying, but he seemed to glow. I liked her better for her consideration. She wasn't all hell cat.

"Cover him and yourself," I told her. "Stay out of sight. I will need to be unfettered."

She glanced at me and nodded. She unrolled Jabeer's blanket and spread it over him.

"No," he protested weakly.

"Don't argue with me or I'll kiss more than your hand."

"You don't understand. That carpet—"

She knelt down and kissed his sallow cheek. He shut up. He might be heading for hell, but he was halfway to heaven at the moment. She was giving him a proper send-off.

I moved to another section and gathered a pile of stones, sticks, and bones. My pride was the thighbone of a camel, a really solid instrument. I know our chances were small, but if things worked out even halfway decently, I would get us through this crisis.

The horsemen did not keep us waiting long. "Master, they come," Faddy whispered.

"Stay out of this," I said. "They aren't going to fall for any of your illusions this time. It's purely up to me. If I get taken out, do what you can for Jewel and Jabeer."

"Hear and obey," he agreed sadly.

The raiders spotted me, which wasn't surprising because I was standing up and waving to them. But they were professionally cautious, having been fooled before. My beckoning figure could be an illusion to cover our retreat. They spread out so as to check other parts of the oasis simultaneously, and one hung back so as to spot anyone who tried to sneak out. They knew what they were doing.

But they hadn't come up against Aladdin before. They had a lesson coming.

My horseman charged in, scimitar lifted. I stood my ground. When he got within range, I hurled my first rock. It missed to the right. By Allah the Magnificent! I was out of practice. I cast the second stone. It missed to the left. Seeing that, the man let out a guffaw.

My third missile caught him on the chest. It surely stung, but did no real damage. Curse again! I had aimed for the neck, where it would crush his larynx and stop his breathing.

Now assured that I was little if any threat to him, he ran his horse directly at me, trying to knock me down. But I had had experience with horses. I stepped aside at the last instant, leaped up, and smacked him across his ugly face with the big solid leg bone. He toppled backward off his mount and landed hard on his scrawny little rear.

I was on him before he could get to his feet, bashing him again with the bone. I felt his skull crack as I laid into it. He was out before he even emitted a productive curse.

I picked up the fallen scimitar and hefted it. It was a good weapon, well balanced, with a sharp edge. Good enough.

"You did it!" Jewel called, evidently relieved.

"Stay clear, woman. It's not yet over."

Now two more raiders headed for me, having seen the fate of their companion. They aligned their steeds and came at me as a pair, spaced just far enough apart so that I could not swing my weapon at both together. I might get one, but the other would get me. Evidently they had had experience with armed pedestrians. They were not common ruffians, but trained warriors. But had they been trained enough?

Time for the second lesson. I showed no fear and made no effort to flee. I stood unmoving, holding my scimitar before me as if to ward them off. That stance should have suggested caution. Like fools, they did not heed it.

The two horses bore down on me like juggernauts, ready to knock me down and trample me without breaking stride. Just as they seemed about to strike me, I made a kind of hissing whistling sound.

Both horses reared back, throwing off their riders and galloping away, terrified.

I went for the nearer man, but he was already on his feet with his scimitar raised, and the other was close behind. Smite me for an infidel! I had hoped to see at least one incapacitated. Only a fool would take on two together.

"I have the second," Jewel called, sweeping in to join the fray.

I opened my mouth, but it was too late to warn her back. She wanted to help me fight? Utter folly! The second man would not kill her outright; he would merely knock her out, bind her, and make his best effort to rape her to death. I had sought to spare her that.

But at the moment I had to focus on my own man. Our scimitars crossed, and I knew immediately that he was no amateur. He attacked me with precision, not leaving himself open to a countersweep.

But I had been trained by the best. I played dumb, backing off, barely fending off his cuts, seeming to tire. Then, just as he thought to finish me off, he got careless. There was my opening.

In a moment his head was rolling on the ground, his body still standing.

I turned immediately to tackle the second. But he was already down in a pool of blood. Jewel was putting her robe back on; I caught only a glimpse of phenomenal breasts. I realized that she had flung her robe off, bracing the man naked, stepping into him with seeming eagerness, and gutted him before he even knew she carried a knife. She had a body to die for, literally.

"Good job," I told her gruffly.

"Thank you. You too. I did not know you were a swordsman."

"You didn't ask."

"What made those horses spook?"

"Little trick I developed long ago. I emulated the whistle of an annoyed basilisk. Few men recognize it, as they are normally dead seconds after they hear it, but horses know it. They knew they would die if they stepped on it. They acted instinctively."

She smiled. "I could get to like you, if I tried."

"Same here. It's a gut thing. But there's one to go."

But there wasn't. The fourth rider, seeing the fate of the others, was racing away.

"Son of a leprous cur!" I swore. "He'll carry the word back, and twice as many will be on our tail in hours."

"So we had better get moving," Jewel said. "Fortunately we now have three fine fresh horses, and the supplies they carry, like food and water."

"Good point," I agreed. "Let's see to Jabeer."

But Jabeer was now beyond hope of recovery. "You tried to warn me," he gasped. "To save me. I want you to have my carpet."

"Oh, I wouldn't take your rug," I protested.

"Take it! Use it! You must! It's—" But he was unable to finish. He choked, shuddered, and died.

"We'll have to bury him," Jewel said sadly.

"Yes. What was he trying to say about his carpet? It looks nice enough, but surely he would prefer to have it with him in the afterlife. We should bury it with him."

"I'm not sure of that," she said. "There was something he said once. I thought he was joking, but maybe he wasn't."

"What did he say?"

"That it's magic."

"She's right, Master," Faddy murmured in my ear. "It is a flying carpet. I recognize the weave. This is a rare gift indeed."

I stared at it. Could this be true?

CHAPTER FIVE

We buried Jabeer in a shallow grave, using the flat blades of the curved scimitars as shovels. Luckily, the sand was loose, which made burying easy. Unfortunately, it would also make excavating his body that much easier for the desert critters.

Hopefully, the three dead soldiers would keep such critters satiated, and leave Jabeer alone, although I did not hold out much hope for that.

Jewel wept for her old friend, but as soon as we were packed and mounted on the soldiers' fine war horses, her cheeks were dry and her jaw was set determinedly.

The oasis wouldn't be safe, not now. In fact, not much in this area would be safe. There were reports of fierce nomadic tribes that made sport of wayward travelers; that is, using their heads in wretched games. Or so people claimed. There were also reports that hidden within these foothills was a secret gateway to the land of djinn. A portal, as some called it, that led to a wondrous, fantastical, verdant land with all sorts of magical creatures. I had my doubts, although Faddy seemed to believe this account, too. As far as I knew, the ifrit had never seen such a land, having little memory of his existence prior to being bound to his ring since its creation eons ago. The very ring that now rested upon my right index finger. Nomadic warriors or not, magical lands or not, we needed to get away from the oasis and take our chances in the hills.

And so, with the sun setting beyond the western landscape, we followed a rocky path that sometimes appeared through the sandy dunes, a path that led toward the shimmering, distant foothills.

Once, in the far distance behind us, I saw a troop of soldiers appear. I immediately led the way around a rare rocky outcropping, but was pleased to see the soldiers take a different path, one that led back toward the outpost from which we had come.

I summoned Faddy immediately, suspecting the ifrit had had something to do with this. I expressed my suspicions, and the lesser djinn confirmed them, unable to lie to me.

"I erased your tracks, master, and, instead created a false trail, one that leads back to Al Bura."

"I thought I told you to leave well enough alone," I whispered to him.

"If you would like, I could remove the false trail and lead the soldiers back here."

I sighed. I had made it a point long ago to use the djinn as little as possible. Often, not all went as planned, and sometimes the ifrit fouled up more than he helped. Besides, it was not good for a man to rely so heavily on such a creature. It made a man less sharp, less resourceful, and less a man.

"No, you did good, Faddy. Thank you."

Faddy did not often physically appear, but when he did it was usually as a young man. He would not appear in this situation, as his existence would be difficult to explain to Jewel, and I rarely spoke of my djinn to anyone. After all, men would kill for such a helpful being. Or, as some would call him, a slave. I did not treat Faddy as a slave. All beings, magical or not, deserved fair treatment. I did not know what powerful magics kept him bound to the ring, but that did not mean I had to make his existence a miserable one. Faddy once confided to me that some of his masters had not been so considerate, and that he had done things he wished to forget.

"Since I have you here, Faddy," I said, "could you confirm that we are on the right course to find the back road."

"Your wish is my command."

"Oh, *please.*"

"I shall return shortly, master."

I gritted my teeth at being called master, but let it slide. I was not a master. I was just a man with a magic ring.

A man, of course, who had once been king.

I shook my head and let the thought go. The thought was a painful one, and it brought up emotions in me that I wanted to forget.

Behind me trailed three of the horses. They would need water as well. It would be best to leave behind such horses, true, but even I could not treat a creature so cruelly. I would not let a living creature die of thirst in such a wasteland, and the oasis we had just left would not support such creatures for very long. For better or for worse, they would trek with us until we found a suitable place to leave them behind.

Remarkably, Jewel took the lead, looking back often and urging me on. If the woman lacked anything, it was patience. I complied, not wishing to face her fury, snapping the reins of my fine mount, and pulling along the trailing pack horses.

Faddy returned shortly, appearing invisibly by my side. "Stay upon this rocky trail, and you will soon come upon a wider road, one that will lead through the mountains."

"And eventually to Samarkand?"

"Yes, master."

Samarkand had a reputation, one that I had not heeded, and for that I have suffered ever since. For it was there that my wife and child were killed. It was there that my life came crumbling down around me. It was there that everything changed, and not for the better.

It was there, after all, that I abandoned my kingdom, and my people.

We continued on, and as the sun dipped below the approaching foothills, I convinced Jewel that we must make camp, or risk breaking a horse's ankle. The horse's ankle did not seem to concern her much, until I reminded her that if we traveled on foot we would, more than likely, never make it out of the desert alive.

She didn't like it, but she acquiesced.

We made camp under a sheltering rock overhang, at the base of the first of a series of foothills that would lead higher and higher until at last we were traveling through mountainous crags. For now, we found some comfort and protection from the cold wind that whipped to life with the setting of the sun.

I provided the horses with some of our valuable water, knowing full well that our supply of it would not last for long. I resisted the urge to ask Faddy to scout ahead. I would soon find out for myself what lay beyond.

As a moderate wind, alternately hot and cold, wound its way over the empty hillside, I made a small fire beneath the overhang, certain it would be shielded from curious eyes, although it was hard to imagine anyone else out here. At least, anyone sane.

The woman was proving to be more trouble than she was worth. A single gold coin hardly seemed worth attacks from heavily armed soldiers and risking one's life in these empty quarters.

As I added fuel to the fire—dry desert grass and the occasional twigs—she watched me from the far recess of the overhang. I felt her eyes one me as I rummaged through the soldiers' bag and found dried meats and dates. I handed some to her and she simply glanced at them, unconcerned.

"You should eat," I said.

"No, I should be searching for my son."

I thought about that, gnawing on what I assumed was dried beef. Then again, it could have been anything. My stomach didn't seem to mind, either way.

"Your son is in Samarkand with his father, is he not?"

She nodded but did not look at me. Her fingers twitched and seemed about to reach for the food, but she seemed too troubled to eat. She would eat when she was hungry enough.

I said, "So he is safe then, no?"

Now she looked at me, turning her full gaze at me. Her flashing almond-shaped eyes caught the firelight and returned it to me a thousandfold. "He is most certainly *not* safe." Her voice shook, and I saw her clawed hand scoop some loose desert sand.

"But he is with his fath—"

"His father has no concern for his safety. Trust me."

The wind picked up. Sand sprinkled over me, and a low moan came from seemingly everywhere. The small hair on my neck stood on end. I knew the sound and I knew the feeling. There were old spirits here. Whether good or ill, remained to be seen.

I was now working on my first date. Still, she had not touched her food. The horses along the perimeter snorted. They would make for a good warning system. Faddy would, too, for that matter, if I commanded him to. For now, I would use the horses.

"Tell me about his father," I said.

"I would rather not."

I leaned back on an elbow near the fire. Jewel, I noticed, was about as far away from me as she could get. Did I smell that bad? I closed my eyes and listened to the fire crackle.

I know a thing or two about people. Ignore them long enough and it's all you can do to shut them up later. I waited, exhausted, close to sleep, when she finally spoke.

"His father is the son of a sheik," she said. "I was the daughter of an important amir, and our families agreed our union would be a good one."

"So you did not marry for love?"

"Does anyone?"

I thought of my dead wife, a woman I had loved more than life itself, and said nothing on that score.

"Go on," I said.

"We had a son and we had a good life. Money, servants, a beautiful home at the edge of a resplendent lake. We had the finest things but, apparently, it was not enough for my ex-husband."

She explained further. Her husband, who had proven to be quite cruel, had always been inclined toward more and more power. Eventually his father was found dead, and her husband—Amir Ibrahim—had immediately assumed control of the vast tribe. But Jewel had always suspected her husband had murdered his own father to gain control. Now, of course, she was certain of it.

"But that does not explain why he would be a threat to his own son," I said. I had sat up at this point. She was sitting forward, too, not quite as morose as before, but certainly not a woman with any joy in her heart.

She smiled bitterly. "My ex-husband, it seems, will stop at nothing to gain power."

"What does that mean?"

"He has made a deal with the devil."

"I don't understand."

"By this time tomorrow night, he will offer up his own son as a blood sacrifice."

I sat straighter. I was not sure I had heard her correctly. "Did you say a sacrifice?"

But she was not looking at me. She had retreated deeper within herself and now I was beginning to sense the reason for her extreme haste.

She said, "I only found out about it days before, from one who had shown kindness to me during my imprisonment."

"We are at least a three day's ride to Samarkand," I said, and then added, "My lady," since I knew now she was of royalty.

"Don't *my lady* me. Out here, I'm not a lady. I'm a mother, and one way or another we *will* reach my son in time."

She sat back and closed her eyes, and as the desert wind whipped into something alive and angry, as our small fire danced in our protective shelter, I suddenly had no doubt that we would, indeed, reach Samarkand.

Except I didn't have any clue how.

CHAPTER SIX

Jewel stirred. "I'm turning in. You will get us there tomorrow."

I nodded numbly. Unable to come up with a viable plan, I focused on a small thing: would she strip to wash herself with some of our limited water before she slept? Would she let me look?

No, she merely lay down on the sand and closed her eyes. I realized that her years in prison must have accustomed her to roughing it. She surely didn't like sleeping dirty, but she could handle it.

Vaguely disappointed, I returned to thoughts of the mission. We had three days riding to accomplish in only one day. That was impossible without magic.

Magic. I didn't like using it much more than Jewel liked roughing it, but I could afford such scruples no more than she could. I touched my ring.

"Master."

"How can we travel three days in one?"

"Are you forgetting the flying carpet, master?"

The carpet! "That can do it?"

"No, master. The average carpet is little faster than a camel. You could travel continuously day and night, but it wouldn't be enough."

"Then what use is it?" I demanded petulantly.

"It will take you to the portal in the foothills."

"Portal?"

"Master, are you teasing me by pretending to be stupid?"

"Who's pretending?"

Faddy sighed. "The portal to Djinnland. Only there will you get the answers and power you need."

"What answers and power?"

"The ones the Djinn of the Lamp will provide."

"That djinn is nonfunctional. I haven't been able to raise him in months."

"Precisely, master. He must obey the call of the Lamp, just as I must obey the summons of the Ring. The fact that he no longer does indicates that he has been made captive in his own realm. You will have to go there and rescue him. Then he will be able to rescue you."

"Me rescue the Djinn of the Lamp? He's a hundred times as powerful as I ever dreamed of being."

"More like a thousand times, master. He's a king among ifrits, while I am but a peon. He must be in dire straits."

"Even if such a feat were possible, we don't have the time. We have only one day!"

"That's why you need him, master. He can do heavy lifting I can't even approach. He can get you to Samarkand almost instantly."

This was ludicrous, but also intriguing. Faddy was not given to lying to me. He was right that the Djinn of the Lamp could solve my problems. But how could I ever hope to solve the Djinn's problems? "I remain almost terminally ignorant. How can I take time off to try to rescue the djinn, when I don't have time for my own mission?"

"That is no problem, master. Time is different in Djinnland. You could spend weeks there, and when you return here, no time will have passed here."

"I'm having trouble believing this."

"It gets worse, master. It's the same way for the djinn. The time we spend in the mortal realm is as nothing in Djinnland. If I ever get to go home, after millennia here, I will arrive there the same time as I left."

"Impossible!"

"No, merely relativistic, master."

"I do not know this word."

"Naturally not, master. It dates from a millennium in your future."

"My future!"

"It would be complicated to explain, master."

I cudgeled my balky brain to focus on immediacies. "So we go to this portal and into Djinnland and rescue Lamprey. Then he rescues us. Exactly how do we rescue him once we're there?"

"That I can't tell you, master. Only that there must be a way. There usually is."

"Thanks a lot!"

He was immune to irony. "Welcome, master."

"How is it you know so much about Djinnland, since you've never been there?"

"I have been there, master. I once lived there. You merely assumed I had not, and I did not correct you, as you had no need to know."

Now I sighed. First things first. "So in the morning we take the flying carpet to the portal."

"Exactly, master."

"Begone."

But at least now I had an approach, crazy as it might be in several ways. I sank into sleep.

Jewel was up before me in the morning, fixing our breakfast. "You didn't try to join me in the night."

"Should I have?"

"No. But I thought you might. Men do get ideas."

"I don't want to get gutted before I complete our mission."

"Is that the whole truth?"

"No. But it will do. Your body does appeal to me. If you ever actually want my attention, you may come to me without your knife and beg me for it."

She smiled, accepting that. I doubted she had ever begged a man for it, or ever would. She thought I feared her retaliation. Just as well, because her antipathy to intimacy was convenient for me. It enabled me to hide the fact that I probably couldn't do anything with her even if she were willing. Because I was impotent, and had been since the death of my wife. I had tried often enough with some quite lovely young women, and succeeded only in embarrassing myself. I had also tried potions and spells, but none were effective. Until I had the cure, whatever it might be, I could do it only verbally. Meanwhile it was not something I cared to discuss with her.

"So how do we get to Samarkand today?" she asked as we finished eating.

"We ride the flying carpet to the portal in the haunted foothills, then enter a portal to Djinnland, where we will rescue a spirit who will get us to Samarkand on time."

She gazed at me. "You believe this?" She had the grace not to add the word "nonsense" but it was hovering there.

"Trust me."

"Do you know how to operate that carpet?"

"No. But it can't be complicated."

She realized she had no choice. "Let's get on with it."

I unrolled the carpet and sat on it. "Go," I said.

Nothing happened.

"Forward," I added.

The carpet took off so suddenly that it dumped me in the sand on my rear. Deprived of its rider, it looped in the air and dropped to the ground.

Jewel was plainly stifling her burgeoning mirth. "Perhaps I should try it."

"Try it," I agreed ungraciously. I did not add the appellation "she-dog," but let it hover there beside her unvoiced word.

She fetched the carpet, spread it flat, sat on it, and spoke almost inaudibly. The carpet lifted, then moved slowly forward, carrying her. She glanced back at me. "Nothing to it."

It turned out that there were a number of specific commands the carpet understood, but it tended to take them literally. When I had told it to go forward, I had not cautioned it to do so slowly. We practiced, and soon got the hang of it.

"What about the horses?" Jewel asked.

"There's a bit of grazing here. We'll try to send someone back for them."

We sat together on the carpet, Jewel first, I with my spread thighs close behind her, clasping her hips. By Allah, her body was winsome! But the one part of my own body that might have taken advantage of that remained fallow. It was frustrating, even though I had no intention of trying anything anyway. I wanted her to think my abstinence was manly courtesy, rather than inability.

"You're impotent," she said.

She must have sat like this with a man before. What could I do but admit it? "Since I lost my wife."

"You must have loved her deeply."

"I did. And my son."

"I know about losing a son. Save mine, and I will see what I can do for you."

I couldn't think of anything smart to say, so I remained silent. If she could actually cure my incapacity, our relationship would suffer a fundamental change. She was an imperious, violent, deadly woman, but I was coming to appreciate her qualities.

She murmured to the carpet, and it lifted and moved forward, slowly accelerating. Soon we were at treetop height and moving swiftly.

I touched my ring. "Guide us," I murmured.

"What?" Jewel asked.

"You might as well know this too," I said with resignation. "I have a minor ifrit named Faddy bound to my ring. He will guide us to the portal."

"You continue to be a man of surprises."

Flying was faster than riding the horses, partly because crags and ravines did not interfere. Before long we reached the site of the portal. There was a hut right where Faddy indicated the portal was. That was surely by no coincidence.

An old robed man stood before the hut as we glided in for a landing. "You are looking for the portal," he said, seeming unsurprised by our appearance. "I am Abu Bakr. I am here to warn you away from it."

We got off the carpet. "I am Niddala, and this is Jewel," I said. "We have urgent need to pass through the portal."

Bakr contemplated me with uncannily perceptive old eyes. I knew in that moment that he recognized me as the former king. Maybe he was a historian. "In that case, there are things you need to know, Niddala."

Good, he was honoring my privacy. "We will appreciate learning them," I said.

"Come in to my abode."

We followed him in. It was much better kept inside than it looked from the outside. Bakr, also, was protecting his privacy.

"We are in a hurry," Jewel said.

"Obviously," Bakr agreed. "But you will get nowhere unless you are sufficiently prepared. Do you know anything about Djinnland?"

"No," I said.

"It is in certain respects the reverse of the mortal realm. We are solid, while the jinn are gaseous. They can assume solidity when they concentrate, but it is not their natural state. In their realm they seem solid, but it is deceptive. Mortals who go there look the same, but are actually enormously denser. As a result, they tend to sink into the ground until they encounter bedrock, and they can not climb trees or ascend to second stories. They can however become diffuse if they focus on that, though they will revert to solidity when they stop focusing. They don't change visibly, but dissipate most of their mass. The opposite of what the jinn do in the mortal realm to become solid. So this has disadvantages as well as advantages."

"Advantages?" I asked.

"In that realm, you will be virtually invulnerable to any attack or weapons they mount against you. Their spears will bounce off you harmlessly. Only when you diffuse to their lesser density will you become vulnerable. They may be lurking to pounce at that moment."

"So we'll stay dense," I said.

"Even then you are not completely safe. Just as King Solomon caught and bound many jinn, a good djinn sorcerer can catch and bind mortal souls in that realm." He glanced at Jewel. "You would be subject to the whim of the possessor of the ring you got bound to, obliged to sate his lust perpetually, unable even to voice objection. You would have to seem to want it, lest you be cruelly punished."

"But the jinni can assume any form they want to," Jewel protested. "Their females are always ravishingly beautiful. Why would they care about my form?"

"Not so," Bakr said. "Their forms are ordinary, and they change them only when they focus. They use illusion to enhance themselves. But the males can see through that illusion. Illusion is like clothing; without it they are naked. But your form is natural, requiring no enhancement by illusion. You would be an invaluable possession, once bound."

Jewel nodded, appreciating the problem. But her determination was unchanged. "We're going in."

"We'll try to stay clear of their sorcerers," I said, though I felt a chill. This would be no picnic.

CHAPTER SEVEN

Before we departed, Bakr fed us a simple stew in his simple abode. His was a solitary life, and one I would not want. True, living at the portal probably offered some adventure; after all, who knew what ilk poured in and out of this magical land? Perhaps *pour* is too strong of a word. I suspected that travelers were rare to the portal. Bakr had seemed truly surprised to see us, and after listening to his alarming warning, I could see why. Human mortals, it seemed, did not fare well in Djinnland.

As Jewel sopped up the rest of her meal hungrily, wiping her bowl clean with a stale piece of bread, I found myself wondering why I was risking life and limb to help a woman I barely knew? True, her gold would come in handy, but hers was certainly not the only paying job. Her beauty was undeniable, but little good that did me. Her beauty, if anything, amplified my shortcomings.

Her son was missing, and that hit home with me. Worse, someone the son had trusted—his very father—was the source of his threat. A father, it seemed, who was not against using the darkest magic to wrest the very kingdom I had once ruled.

Perhaps it was time for me to come out of my self exile? Perhaps it was time for me to move on?

Perhaps.

When we were finished, Bakr provided us with some provisions, reiterated some of his most dire warnings, and pointed us to the portal, which, as it turned out, was a rock bridge that spanned a wide chasm. The bridge disappeared into roiling mist, and what awaited us beyond, I could only guess.

I thought we needed to travel light, so I left my incidental belongings, including the little chest, with Bakr. That chest contained the Lamp, which I felt would be useless in Djinnland. I had to trust the sage not to molest my things. If by some mischance I did not return, then maybe he would be a deserving inheritor of the Lamp.

"No, take it with you," Jewel murmured.

She had caught on? She was almost too smart. I opened the chest, removed the lamp, fitted it in a pocket, and closed the chest again.

Bakr assured me that he would fetch our mounts and take care of them, as he could always use them to barter with future travelers. And with the sun high above and our bellies full, Jewel and I set out along a narrow rock path which led from his hut. I carried over my shoulder a satchel full of provisions, rolled up the magic carpet, and strapped it down to our bag. A thrill of excitement coursed through me. Perhaps I should have been wary. Perhaps I should have been overly cautious. But I was never one to run from danger, and I was never one to leave a woman without hope. Especially a beautiful woman who was already stirring curious emotions inside me. Emotions that I had thought were long dead.

Jewel and I soon crossed a wide section of desert, following a curiously raised rock trail that led directly to the arching bridge. At the foot bridge, I was suddenly a mixture of apprehension and excitement. A hot wind swept up from the chasm, thundering over us, hot enough to seemingly sear my eyebrows.

Next to me, Jewel peered over the edge of the cliff. Her hair whipped about her face crazily, and if she was afraid, she didn't show it. I joined her at the edge and looked as well. More mist, roiling and churning far below. It would be a long, long drop. To where, I had no clue. Perhaps the djinn underworld, if there was such a place.

The world is full of magic, if one chooses to look. In my case, magic always seemed to find me.

I stepped back, suddenly dizzy. I rubbed my ring. "Will you guide us, Faddy, once we are in Djinnland?"

His voice came to me instantly, although it was nearly drowned out by the hot wind roaring up from below. "I should warn you, master, that I am not bound to you in this magical land."

"Why is that?"

"This is my natural home, master. The magic is reversed."

"So we could be bound to a powerful sorcerer, then."

"Yes, Bakr spoke the truth."

"Could we be bound to you?"

"I am not a powerful enough sorcerer, master."

"Will you help us once we are there?"

"Will you someday free me?"

"I have always planned to someday free you."

"Then I will see what I can do for you, master."

"And, for the love of Allah, please stop calling me master."

"In Djinnland, you will not be my master, master."

I groaned.

"Are you speaking to your ifrit?" asked Jewel, joining me a few feet from the cliff's edge. Her long, black hair had been blown in every which way. She looked as if she had spent a wild night making love. A pleasant if not disheartening thought. After all, it could never be me making love.

"Yes," I said to her. "I'm seeking some last-minute guidance." To Faddy, I asked, "How do we make ourselves 'less dense'?"

"It is a state of mind, master. It is a matter of will power. Hold tight to an image of yourself floating, even if you find yourself sinking. Hold fast and do not let it go."

"Sounds easy enough."

"Unless you are distracted."

"Then let's pray for minor distractions."

I relayed this information to Jewel and she merely nodded, as if this was something she already suspected she must do in Djinnland. To Faddy, I probed further, "How big is this land?"

"Massive. I have never seen the end of it."

"And how do we find our trapped djinn?"

"Of this, I do not know. But perhaps I know someone who could help. An elder djinn."

"Will you lead us to him?"

There was a slight pause. "Yes, master."

"Thank you, Faddy. Be gone."

"Are we ready?" asked Jewel.

"I think so."

We stepped up onto the stone bridge, and almost immediately I knew something was different. The magical connection with Faddy was broken.

"El Fadl?" I called, but there was no response. My ifrit, for now, was free.

"He is gone?" asked Jewel, her sharp mind grasping the situation immediately.

I nodded, feeling oddly alone and vulnerable. I had forgotten just how much I had come to rely on my simple ifrit.

We continued onto the arching bridge, which angled up high and was far narrower than I had hoped. A hand rail would have been nice, too, but we had no such luck. I didn't have a fear of heights, but walking over something like this wasn't easy. And the bedeviled wind, which thundered over us like banshees escaping from the netherworld below, didn't make things any easier.

But we plowed along, with myself in the lead. Despite her apparent fearlessness, Jewel reached forward and took my hand. I gave it to her willingly, pleased to be wanted in such an intimate way, and led the way up the curving strip of bridge. When we reached the apex of the stone structure, something strange began to happen.

Strange, but not unexpected, since we had been warned.

Each step grew more and more difficult. Our bodies were growing denser and it was a strange feeling, indeed. Jewel gripped my hand even tighter, and I saw her struggling as well. I reassured her as best as I could, but, for the most part, I shared her unease.

As we continued down the bridge, we came to a stretch that was riddled with holes wide enough for a man to fall through. The bridge, apparently, was falling apart. I halted and tested the surrounding stones. They seemed to hold, and just as I was about to navigate around the holes, Jewel yanked hard on my hand.

"We are growing heavier and heavier, as Bakr warned. Perhaps other adventurers did not receive such a warning."

I looked again at the gaping voids in the bridge. "Or perhaps they didn't heed his warnings." I nearly attempted to summon Faddy but stopped myself. "I think, perhaps, we better think lighter thoughts."

"But how? I do not feel so light now."

I knew what she meant. With my legs trembling from the weight of my upper body, thinking light thoughts seemed a near impossibility. As I thought about how to approach the problem, I found myself gazing ahead at the swirling mist that awaited us in Djinnland. The wispy mist. Roiling. Churning. So light.

"Something's happening," said Jewel behind me.

I turned and found her staring at me open-mouthed. "What?"

She pointed. "You're doing it, but how?"

"Doing what?"

"I can see *through* you, Niddala. But how? I feel as heavy as a birthing elephant."

I held up my arms in wonder, staring at them. Indeed, I could see through them. Also, the sense of heaviness had abated, but now it was returning, and I soon felt the crushing weight.

The mist! I quickly told her about it, instructing her to hold the swirling fog front and center in her thoughts. She did so, as did I, and soon we could both see through the other. I found myself wishing I could see through her clothing, as well, but no such luck.

Holding her hand, I led the way safely down over the bridge, bypassing the gaping holes, and to the waiting mist below.

Djinnland.

CHAPTER EIGHT

Ahead of us the raised rock trail continued, curving into the mist. Where did it lead?

I rubbed my ring, but there was no response. That made me uncomfortable, though I knew Faddy did not have to respond, because he had said he would guide us. Was he reneging? I did not think so. Then why was he not here?

Jewel tested the path with her foot. “Seems solid,” she said. “But does it go where we need to go?”

“I don’t trust it,” I said. “It must go where the jinn want it to. That could be a trap for unwary visitors.”

“They can’t get many visitors. More likely they use it themselves. Ask your ifrit; he surely knows.”

“He’s not responding.”

“Then how do we know where we need to be?”

“It’s a problem,” I agreed.

“I have an ugly thought.”

“Faddy wouldn’t betray us. I’ve known him for years and he’s a good person, for an ifrit.”

“Not about Fatty.” She paused, but I did not correct her, knowing she was teasing me. “About whoever has captured your other ifrit.”

“I call him Lamprey. That’s not his name, but it serves.”

“Lamprey,” she agreed. “Whoever has him may actually be after you. This is his way of making you come to him.”

I whistled. “Could be! Bait for the trap. But why would a powerful jinn want me?”

"I don't know, but he must have a reason."

"None that I can fathom. It seems like way more effort than it's worth."

"Think of my ex husband."

I did, getting her point. Jewel might be nothing in herself, but she had motive to rescue their son, and that made her a threat to the man's demonic designs. So he watched her, and acted the moment she did. After the boy had been sacrificed Jewel could probably be ignored, but right now he was not stinting in his effort to keep her away.

Similarly, I might be a threat to the djinn leader, so he was acting to take me out. There would be no evidence if it happened in Djinnland. What threat was I to him? Well, I had been king, and might one day be again. Kings had power, as I well knew, and I did know how to use it, and would if I had reason. Maybe he needed to be certain I never recovered that power.

"Then I think we had better stay out of sight," I said. "We may be up against things we have no inkling of."

"Exactly."

"It occurs to me that this could be why Faddy is not answering. He knows they are watching him, and want him to lead them to us. So he is staying away, lest he betray me simply by responding."

"Couldn't they find us as simply by watching the bridge?"

"You'd think so. Maybe there's magic on it that conceals who crosses."

"That mist."

"That mist," I agreed. "But we'll be clear enough the moment we leave it."

"So what do we do?"

I pondered and came up with a devious plan. "Time is static here. That is, no matter how long our mission takes, no time will pass for us in the mortal realm. So we don't have to hurry. We can take a year if we need to."

"A year!"

"Better to take that time, than walk into a trap."

She nodded. "We do have time."

"We can take the most devious unlikely route, where they won't have spies out, then strike suddenly when we spy our objective."

"Devious route to *where?*"

"We'll just have to find Lamprey ourselves. We'll look for the most impressive djinn estate and see if he's there. Given sufficient time, we can do it."

She eyed me slantwise. "Are you hoping to travel alone with me indefinitely?"

"That might be nice, but no. I want to rescue Lamprey, return to our own realm, rescue your son, then discover how well you like me when you're grateful."

She laughed. "You would like me very well. But first you have to accomplish those other things."

"I will do my best." Then I remembered something. "You made me bring the lamp with me. Why?"

"Lamprey must normally live inside the lamp, to be immediately at hand when you summon him."

"True," I agreed. I had not thought of that before. "He is bound magically to the lamp, unless I send him off."

"And you sent him off?"

I thought of my dead wife and child. After their deaths years ago, I had abandoned everything. Yes, I had sent my genie off. I wanted solitude and peace, and I would have sent Faddy off, too, if I hadn't forgotten about the ring. It had been months later into my self-exile that I had come upon the ring among my limited belongings. Turns out, Faddy makes for a halfway decent companion.

Jewel seemed about to ask why I had sent the genie off, but thought better of it. Perhaps she would ask at another time. Instead, she said, "So the lamp must be a safe place for him."

"It must be," I agreed. What was she getting at?

"He must be able to zero in on it at all times, so he doesn't get lost when performing some foolish distant task you set him to."

"Yes." Again I had not thought of that.

"So maybe it also orients on him. Maybe you can use it to get a line on him."

My stupid jaw dropped. "Maybe so," I agreed.

I brought out the lamp. It was a dull brass, really rather ordinary. I touched its side.

The side was warm. Startled, I touched the other side. It was cool. "I'll be an infidel's grandson!" I swore. "It's signaling his direction!"

"I thought it might. Now how are we going to get to him without being discovered? I don't want to be caught and bound to a horny jinn stud forever."

It was time for me to strategize. "First, concealment," I said. "Are you claustrophobic?"

"What does that have to do with this?"

"Trust me."

"No, I'm not claustrophobic."

"Good. Because it will be close and dark where we're going."

"Where is that?"

"Underground."

"I don't understand."

I was pleased to be leading her mind, instead of having her lead mine. "First, we revert to full solidity. That means we can't be harmed by their weapons, which is good. It also means we have to walk on bedrock, because nothing else will sustain us."

"And your point is?"

"Bedrock generally runs some distance below ordinary ground. You can't see through ground. It's excellent concealment."

"How will we breathe?"

Good question. Maybe too good. "I'm betting that in our solid state, ordinary ground will be almost as tenuous as air, and there is air between the clods. I'm betting we can breathe. If not, I'll think of something else."

"How will we find any castles when we're below ground?"

"Castles generally sit on bedrock."

"If we locate Lamprey, how will we get him out of there?"

"We'll bash out a wall and break his manacles and turn him loose. We don't need to take him anywhere, just free him; I can summon him later with the lamp."

She gazed at me with something that on a better day might almost be mistaken for approval. "You have a mind like a fox."

"Thank you." I really did appreciate her respect.

"But wouldn't it be easier and safer simply to put him in the lamp? It's as solid as we are, so should be protection against their efforts to recover him, as long as we protect it."

Now I stared at her. "And you have the mind of a vixen."

"Thank you." Then we both smiled. I liked that.

We solidified, which was our natural state here, and waded off the raised path and into the slop that was the ground. Jewel did not seem to feel the dark closure, but I discovered it did bother me. Then my eyes adjusted, and I found there was very dim light that enabled me to see a short distance around me. It was like peering through extremely heavy fog. Mainly I saw the roots of trees reaching down from above, and the rough contours of the bedrock below, with some suspended blobs that were dislodged chunks of bedrock.

And I felt the small warmth of the side of the lamp. I headed that way, stepping carefully because I did not know how treacherous this nether terrain could be. Suppose there were a hole in the bedrock? How deep would it go? How bad could a long fall hurt?

Then the bedrock angled up. That was a relief. When it was near the surface, I signaled caution to Jewel, who was following close behind, and then poked my head carefully up through the surface tension of the ground.

I was amazed. We appeared to be in a rise in a field near a farmstead. What looked like herbivorous dragons were grazing on bright blue grass. The fences were sparkling silver. The house was a lovely tower with multicolored minarets.

"What a beautiful picture," Jewel murmured beside me. Only her head was visible, like mine, above the blue turf. "It must be mostly illusion."

"Illusion?" I asked blankly.

"It's probably an ordinary ratty farm, enhanced to make it look splendid. That's what I would do if I had illusion to spare."

"Every peon becomes a prince," I agreed, seeing it in more than one sense.

"What's that?" Her hand poked out of the ground and pointed to a marked stone.

I looked.

On the surface of the stone was drawn a crude circle containing a crude tower. A line slanted through it. "That's a no-signal," I said. "Meaning stay away from there."

"Why?"

I suffered a flash of brilliance. "Because that's not where we're going. Lamprey is not there. We must look elsewhere."

"How can you tell it means that?"

"Because it has Faddy's signature." I pointed to the crude little fat man drawn below the circle. "He is on duty, informing us without ever leading the enemy to us. He knew we'd pass this way, so he left a message. When we find a signal that tells us to go there, we'll know we've found it."

"I am getting to like Faddy," she said, this time pronouncing it correctly.

CHAPTER NINE

We had been traveling along the bedrock for some time, slogging through ethereal dirt and tree roots and even glowing subterranean worms that shivered when we passed through them. I shivered, too, fighting my revulsion.

It was hard to believe that just yesterday I had been lounging lazily in my tent, idly wondering if I would ever find work again. Well, I surely found work. And what strange work it was.

We continued for some time. Since it was easy to get lost down here, I kept the lamp in hand, touching it often, adjusting our direction based on the heat signature. Once, we came upon what appeared to be a deep ravine where the bedrock dropped steeply away. Standing on the edge of the bedrock cliff, we debated what to do. We could parallel the edge of the cliff, and search for a section that would ford the bedrock ravine. Or, as Jewel suggested, we could lighten our bodies enough so as not to drop down into the ravine, but not so much as to float entirely up to the surface.

We tried it. I seemed to have a better handle on easily lightening and weighing down my body—aw, men and their vivid imaginations. Jewel struggled a bit, sometimes sinking much deeper than me, or alternately rising much higher. Finally, I took her hand and together we crossed the open space in the bedrock. Shortly, we found ourselves on the dense rock, and we continued forward again, guided by the lamp.

"I'm hungry," said Jewel, as we passed around a colony of long, furry creatures that lived in cozy burrows. I didn't wish to disturb them, and so we skirted their labyrinthine tunnels as best we could.

I was hungry and thirsty, too. As her guide and escort, her hired hand, and as the male, I would be expected to find us food. But what would we eat in this world? We discussed this as we walked.

"Perhaps fruit," said Jewel. I noticed that she often took my hand as we walked over the corrugated bedrock. She made it seem that she needed it to help keep her footing. I also noticed that she did not release it so readily. She held it tightly, and I found her touch reassuring as well. We were, after all, deep beneath a magical world so unlike our own.

"Would fruit nourish us?" I asked. "Wouldn't it be like trying to eat smoke?"

"I would like to see you try to eat smoke," said Jewel, and she swung our interlaced hands. "I could use a good laugh. It has been a long, long time since I laughed deeply. I do not think I can laugh again until I find my boy."

I knew the feeling. I had not laughed deeply since I lost my boy.

I said, "If we raise ourselves to the density of the food, I suspect we can eat it."

"And what happens if we lower our density later? Would the food disappear from our bellies?"

"There is only one way to find out."

We traveled for what I believed were many more hours, although judging time was difficult for obvious reasons. In this respect, our hunger was our time piece, and judging by the way my own hunger gnawed at me, I concluded that a full day had passed since we first left Bakr and entered Djinnland.

By the time the bedrock sloped gently up, our stomachs were growling in unison. It might have been funny if it weren't so uncomfortable. The air around us brightened as we approached the surface. I could only imagine the start we would give a person who saw two heads emerge from the ground. No different than the start spirits and demons gave humans in our physical world, flitting through doorways and walls.

My head appeared above ground first, and I saw that we were in the middle of what must surely pass for night in this world. The golden sky was replaced with a darker, silvery glow. The rocky incline we had been following formed a small, bare mound in the middle of what appeared to be woods. We were surrounded by narrow, translucent trees that pulsed with an inner light. On the ground near my face, presently my eye level, was an array of flat, multi-colored mushrooms. If anything, Djinnland was not lacking for color.

Near a particularly wide mushroom with a glowing purple cap, was Jewel's head poking up through the earth. Her scanning eyes met mine. We were alone, wherever we were. I nodded, and we ascended onto the rocky hillock. As we went, I raised my vibration and lightened myself enough to gather some of the colorful mushrooms.

As we sat together on the hilltop in this strange world, with the silvery sky above and the translucent trees swaying nearby and the distant blasts of fire from what I assumed were more dragons, I probably should have felt fear or, in the least, apprehension. But I didn't. I felt excitement. More excitement than I had ever felt before. I was in a strange and distant land, with a beautiful woman who needed help. What more could an adventurer want?

The air was cool, with a hint of something savory on it. Then again, perhaps anything at this point would seem savory. We both looked down at the mushrooms piled between us.

"Do you think they're safe to eat?" I asked.

"There's no way to know—wait, what's that?"

She pointed to a patch of rock behind me. I turned and looked. It was more writing, written directly onto the stone surface. I stood immediately and moved to it, aware once again of the crushing weight that I brought with me. Already, my ankles felt swollen and the muscles along my legs and back ached.

"It's from Faddy," I reported. Like the first sign, this was a child-like drawing of a rotund man pointing forward. I looked in the direction he was pointing, squinting through the silvery night, and there, in the far distance, was the silhouette of a hulking fortress.

"We go that way," I said motioning toward the fortress. "Lamprey's in there. I'm sure of it."

Indeed, I felt my lamp and it was glowing warmer. We were very, very close.

Jewel, who was standing next to me, pointed at the drawing. "Hey, look what's in his other hand."

I looked and I saw it, too. Jewel picked up a bluish mushroom and took a big bite.

"I guess these are okay, after all. You know, I might just need to get an ifrit of my own. Well, maybe not."

"Why not?" I asked around a mouthful of the mushroom. Unfortunately, the bite didn't last long. After just a few chews, the stuff disappeared in my mouth. I thought lighter thoughts and felt myself grow less dense. I tried another bite and this time I was sable to chew it completely and swallow. I could even feel it sitting there in my appeased stomach. So far, so good.

I could see that Jewel had dissipated slightly, too. In fact, I could even see through her in parts. What a strange world this was.

Jewel continued after adjusting herself enough to accommodate the food. "Well, first of all, they are not easy to come by. And it seems that you not only have one, but two. You must surely be a remarkable man."

I shrugged, grinning. Life has been both kind and painful for me.

"Don't be too pleased, Niddala. Those people I have known who owned such ifrits or djinns, always were lazy and incapable of dealing with life on their own. They came to rely too much on their magical slaves."

I nodded. I knew the temptation well. It was why I had sent Lamprey off, and why I did my best to use Faddy only when I needed him the most.

"Such men I find slothful and disgusting."

"Do you find me slothful and disgusting?" I asked.

She finished off her latest fat mushroom. "So says the man with glowing mushroom remnants in his beard." She grinned at me, letting me know that she was playing. She shrugged. "Slothful? Perhaps not. I have seen you in action, and you need little prodding. Now, how much you have used your ifrit on this journey, I do not know, but you seem like a man capable of making his own decisions and following his own heart. Disgusting? So far, no, but that remains to be seen."

"You have been studying me."

"I have had no choice."

I enjoyed being ribbed by her. "Fair enough," I said.

We gathered more of the mushroom, storing them, of all places, in Lamprey's lamp. We stood together on the stony hillside and looked down on the distant fort. As we stood there, Jewel slipped her hand inside my arm and held on. She had needed no support this time. Indeed, she was holding me because she wanted to. I took in a little air. Her touch was heavenly.

"We can walk there above ground," I said, "if we lighten up."

"But then we risk exposing ourselves to potential threats in this world."

"Unfortunately," came a voice behind us. "You've already done that."

CHAPTER TEN

Both of us whirled, startled. There before the trees stood a swarthy jinn man wearing a scimitar and what appeared to be a coil of rope. I knew he was a jinn, because of the typical arrogant curve of his upper lip and a certain nebulosity of his countenance. Anyway, what else could he be, here in Djinnland? He seemed to be alone, but he looked dismayingly confident. I didn't trust that. I needed to know why he was sure of himself, before I waded into what could be a treacherous encounter. That meant stalling.

"Run, Jewel!" I called. "Don't let him ravish you!"

She caught on instantly. That was another thing I liked about her. "Spare him, honored sir!" she pleaded. "I'll do anything you demand, only let him go unharmed." She opened her shirt, revealing her marvelous frontal curvature.

The jinn paused, as any man of any type would, eying her phenomenal exposure. He recognized of course that her structure was real, not illusion.

"Don't do it!" I cried. "Don't trust him. He'll ravish you then kill me anyway!"

"Forgive me, beloved; I've got to," she said. "I can't bear the thought of you suffering." She stepped toward the jinn, opening her shirt further.

"Forget it, wench," the jinn said. "My master would make me a eunuch if I touched a piece like you. He'll be using you himself, I'm sure, until you wear out." Then he drew not the scimitar but the rope. Was he going to try to tie her up?

Jewel paused in place, bare bosom heaving provocatively, waiting for the man to come to his senses. That was bound to happen soon. Once he embraced her he would be a dead jinn, but he did not know that. How could any man know that, dazzled by her splendor?

The jinn lifted the rope and whirled a loop over his head. What mad game was he playing?

Then he flung the loop not at Jewel, but at me. Surprised, I was slow to react. All I did was step back a pace. But Jewel acted; she leaped to get before me, and the loop settled over her head and shoulders. It wasn't a garrote; it hung on her body loosely. What was the point?

Her expression changed, becoming devoid of fake passion. She looked completely passive. "Do with me what you wish," she told the jinn. "Your will is my will." She did not seem to be pretending. This was extremely odd.

"I don't want *you,* wench!" the jinn snapped. "I want *him.*" He hauled her to him and yanked the rope off her. He stepped back and raised it for another whirl of the loop.

That was when I grabbed him from behind, hugging him hard and lifting him off his feet. Distracted for key moments, he had taken his eyes off me, and I had gotten close enough.

"Grab the rope!" I told Jewel. "Put the loop on him!"

She did so, efficiently.

The jinn ceased all resistance. He had been pacified by the loop.

Jewel closed her shirt. It had served its purpose.

Now we were in business. "Who are you?" I asked.

"I am Morabec, lowly vassal to Prince Zeyn, lord of this kingdom."

"Well, Moron Beck," I said. "Why did you come after me?"

"Prince Zeyn sent me to investigate your appearance by the sacred grove. I was supposed to capture you and bring you to him for interrogation."

"What is Zeyn's interest in me?"

"You are likely the possessor of the Lamp that commands the Ifrit Iften, second in power only to Zeyn himself. If so, you are a key mortal man who will enable Zeyn to take control of the mortal kingdom as well as Djinnland."

"Ludicrous," Jewel exclaimed.

But it wasn't ludicrous. The jinn prince evidently knew my identity as the former king who could return at any time to resume power. Now I knew why he had captured Lampry, or maybe Iften. It was to get control of me, put me back on the throne, and use me to work his will in the mortal realm.

"Assuming this nonsense is true," I said carefully, "Why does he think I would cooperate in betraying my own kingdom?"

"Once you are spelled, your cooperation will be involuntary. If there were any doubt, he could simply torture your paramour here to force your compliance. If that did not suffice, he could cut off your manhood an excruciating sliver at a time. No one says no to Prince Zeyn." He smiled a trifle bitterly. "Not for long, anyway."

Just so. "How did you sneak up on us unawares?"

"I used the magic conduit from the castle to the sacred grove, then stepped out from behind the trees."

"This rope you have—what is it?"

"It is a magic lariat, that my master acquired from a future far western land. It compels any person roped to obey the will of its possessor without resistance or evasion."

I nodded. That could be one useful rope.

"Where is the Ifit Iften imprisoned? In the deepest dungeon?"

"Not at all. Solidified mortals could readily reach that. He is in the topmost turret of the castle, where mortals can't readily go, protected by all manner of traps."

"So how can Iften be rescued?"

"That is beyond my expertise," Morabec said.

"You have no idea?"

"I don't think it can be done."

Aladdin was curious how far the rope would make its captive go. "If you were assigned to do it, how would you proceed?"

"I would send in the lady to persuade Zeyn to let Iften go. But I doubt she could succeed."

That was probably a true assessment. Was their mission doomed?

"What else do we need to know?" Jewel asked Morabec.

"That your time is brief. Soon Zeyn will realize that I am taking too long, and will investigate. Then you will be doomed."

I looked at Jewel. "Do you want to give it up?"

"No! My life is over if I do not save my son."

"Even though you risk sexual slavery if we continue?"

She shook her head. "If Zeyn puts that loop on me, I will be his slave. I have felt its power. He surely has other ways. If he puts the loop on you, you will serve him loyally, and betray the mortal realm." She took a breath. "I will risk it if you will."

It was one huge gamble. But not following up was probably almost as bad, because the jinn prince would track us down before we could escape Djinnland. "We'll try it," I said.

"You have a plan?"

"I have a plan," I agreed, marshaling my lagging brain.

"That's a relief. I would have gutted our captive."

"Sometimes there are better uses for a man than gutting," I said with the thought of a smile.

She responded with her own thought of a smile. "Oh? I am surprised to learn that."

My cudgeled brain began to function. Desperation helped. "Morabec will take us in as captives."

She stared at me. "That's your plan?"

"All will not be quite as it appears," I said. "The loop I wear will be a fake. Morabec will wear the real one, concealed. You of course will be bound by the threat to me, willing to do anything to spare me my fate."

"And what do we do when we are hauled before Zeyn?"

"I haven't worked out that detail yet."

"Well, work it out!"

I drew her away from Morabec. "My suspicion circuit is working. This is too pat. I don't fully trust that loop. It may work on mortals, but may not work on ifrits. If that is the case, Morabec will play along to get us into the castle, then betray us to his master. So when we get there, I want you to slip away while attention is on me, take the flying carpet and sail quietly up to the topmost turret, jam Lamprey into the Lamp, and take off for home. If you get in trouble, densify to the max and try to plow through to the exit."

She nodded. "I suspect similar. But what about you?"

"I'll manage one way or another. I can densify too."

"Allah smite you for a liar! Even so, how would I manage without you?"

"You will have Lamprey. He obeys the holder of the Lamp. He will be all you need to rescue your son."

Her mouth worked for a moment before anything came out. "You—you are sacrificing yourself to enable me to escape and rescue my son?"

"I am trying to enable you to complete your mission. I will take care of myself. Maybe my bluff will be effective, and I'll escape Zeyn's clutches. Meanwhile I'll distract him so you can get the job done."

"I could distract him better."

"Surely so. But you need to be free to rescue your son."

"Why are you doing this, you idiot?

"Because I'm an idiot, as you say."

"Not because you're smitten with me?"

"That too, maybe," I agreed.

She bit her lip, then decided. "We'll try it. If it works, and I rescue my son, I will return for you."

"With luck you won't need to. I'll return on my own."

"With luck," she repeated. "How much luck have you had in the past year?"

"Not much. So I'm about due."

"You're impossible." Suddenly she kissed me. It was amazing how potent she was able to make such a brief experience. "I will make it worth it, for you, if I have the chance."

"Wrap the carpet about your body so it doesn't show. Here is the Lamp."

She wrapped, and took. We were almost ready.

We returned to the captive ifrit. Jewel examined the magic rope, then harvested some fibrous weeds and wove what appeared to be a similar rope. She fitted a loop of this around my waist. It looked authentic. Then she worked the genuine lariat loop under Morabec's shirt so that it did not show. It seemed the ifrit might use illusion to enhance his appearance, but not for actual clothing; the shirt was real. We were ready.

"Act as you normally would, with prisoners," I told Morabec. "Take us to your leader."

"I must say, you have nerve," the jinn said. "You're doomed, but impressive in your folly."

We went to the copse, and found the magic conduit. Morabec spoke the words, and we were suddenly swept across the landscape to the distant fort.

We were there. Now what?

CHAPTER ELEVEN

We were in a wide tunnel. Torches flickered on the stone walls, mounted in small nooks. Behind us was a massive iron gate, and before us, perhaps a hundred feet away, was a heavy wooden door. Standing to either side of the door were heavily armed guards. All were watching us closely.

"You are to act naturally," I commanded Morabec. "You are to act as if you really did capture us."

He nodded. "As you wish."

"Now, lead us as you would normally to your master, and do not give him any indication that things are not as they seem."

He nodded again. "As you wish. And you're sinking."

So I was. The stone floor provided some support for my heavier mass, but not enough. It appeared that only true bedrock could support our bodies fully. Jewel and I adjusted our density levels to comfortably stand on the stone floor. Once done, the ifrit led us down the hall and to the guards.

"I have two prisoners for Lord Zeyn," Morabec announced. I saw no indication of the ifrit doing anything other than his duty, but then again, I was wholly out of my element here. What did I know of magic and the ways of djinns? Not much, although certainly more than the average man, as I presently owned two. For all I knew, a silent message had been successfully passed from him to the guards. If so, I would surely find out soon enough.

But one of the guards simply nodded and stepped aside. The heavy door swung silently open on its own volition. More magic, surely. What chance did we have? Non-magical beings in a land of magic, about to face perhaps the most magical being of them all?

I didn't know, but I wasn't going down without a fight.

Famous last words, I thought.

Morabec entered first, leading me by the non-magical rope Jewel had fastened. I, of course, discreetly held the real magical lariat behind him. Whether the lariat did any good would be revealed soon enough, too. Jewel followed behind, gently holding on to the hem of my shirt. Even that slight touch was heavenly.

I am no better than a young boy with a silly crush.

We entered a grand throne room as befitted the wealthiest of kings. Apparently Zeyn was not only a great magician but a ruler, as well. Perhaps, then, this was nothing more than a heavily fortified palace. Indeed, ifrit guards lined the walls, all watching us, all heavily armed. We traversed the long room, crossing over a thick and ornate carpet.

We approached a raised platform and a beautiful throne. The thing sitting on the throne, however, was anything but beautiful. The powerful ifrit, Zeyn I assumed, was a monster of a man, spilling out of the great chair that would have sat two comfortably. A massive crystal chandelier lit the entire room in a reddish glow. Flying above us were small creatures with long, scaly necks and tales. Small dragons, perhaps. These creatures were largely ignored by everyone in the room. I noticed the creatures were coming into and out of the room through a window high above.

Zeyn was watching us closely. He was also sweating profusely. His red-eyed gaze settled on Jewel and he licked his thick lips. She stepped closer to me.

Zeyn turned his gaze onto me and for the first time in a long time I felt real fear. The man—or djinn—was a monster.

"You are afraid of me," said Zeyn, licking his lips again. "I can sense fear."

I sensed he fed on fear. I sensed that fear, perhaps, served him quite well. Fear gave him added strength, fear enhanced his magical gifts. How I knew this, I didn't know, but I always trusted such feelings. Trusting these feelings have served me well.

I took in a lot of air and fought through my fear. I was King Aladdin, after all. I had ruled a mighty kingdom, and had done so quite well. I feared no man, or ifrit.

Zeyn cocked his head slightly. "The fear is gone. Just like that. Curious, curious." He looked at Jewel. "You have no fear, either. Just loathing for me. You would do well to fear me, my dear, because I am going to be your worst nightmare."

"You are a pig."

One corner of his wide mouth lifted and I assumed this was a grin. A half-hearted attempt if I had ever seen one. Zeyn turned his attention back to me. "It is a pleasure to finally meet you, King Aladdin. It's a shame it had to be under such regretful conditions." He motioned toward the rope that allegedly bound me magically.

Next to me, Jewel gasped. "King Aladdin? What is he talking about, Niddala?"

Now the great magician threw back his mighty head and roared with laughter. Startled, the little dragons perched atop the chandelier took flight. They headed for the dark window above.

"Niddala, is it? How simple, yet clever." He looked at Jewel, who still stood behind me. "Ah, my dear, did you not know that you've been in the presence of the great King Aladdin, protector of the innocent and defenseless, a once mighty ruler who gave up his throne because fortune did not smile down upon him?"

Jewel stepped back and took in a lot of air. I felt her eyes on me. But I did not take my own off the creature in front of me. If anything, I had learned to keep my eyes on my enemies. Never off. Perhaps at another time and place I would have been amused by her shock, but now was not the time.

Zeyn continued, "But your loss is my gain, my lord. Your absence has left a void in the kingdom, and as such there are many who desire to rule your rich lands. Your puppet king substitute, what's his name, Huran, has little power to suppress them. You can count me as one of those."

With Jewel's eyes still on me, I spoke to the disgusting being in front of me. "What does an ifrit want with the lands of man?"

He grinned at me, and this time both corners of his mouth lifted so high that his ears wiggled. He then looked at Jewel and his grin turned into pure, unabashed lust. He licked his lips again. "The answer, my lord, is obvious, isn't it?"

"To appease your lust?"

"Men have fought for far less, as you well know."

Jewel found her voice. "You are not a man. You are something filthy and wretched."

"Something filthy and wretched that you will come to know quite well, my dear. How your husband gave you up, I do not know. Perhaps he was tired of your mouth."

He snapped his fat fingers and an ifrit appeared before us, materializing instantly. Zeyn was about to say something when Jewel spoke again, in shocked surprise.

"You!" she hissed.

The thin man, with hands folded before him and wearing a long colorful robe, smiled and bowed. "We meet again, Emira Jewel."

"Who is he?" I asked, stunned that she would know anyone in this kingdom.

"It is because of him that I found you," said Jewel.

"I do not understand," I said.

"I was searching for help, asking around for someone who could be trusted, and this man appears as if from nowhere and gives me your name and how to find you." She turned back to the ifrit who was smiling pleasantly at us. "But why?"

"I will answer that, my soon to be play thing," said Zeyn. "He did so on my command. You see, I needed to lure your king into my realm, as I have big plans for him. One way to do that was capture his djinn and let fate do the rest. And fate is such a good friend of mine these days."

"Why not just kidnap me?" I said. "Obviously you knew who I was and where to find me."

"Indeed, for you have the djinn's lamp, and the djinn is deeply connected to it. With just a little prodding and perhaps a lot of torture, the djinn gave up his secrets and led us to you. Unfortunately, my strength is not nearly as powerful in your world as it is in mine, and so I could not overpower you."

"You are working with my ex-husband," said Jewel.

"He thinks he is working with me," said Zeyn. "He is proving very valuable and nearly as wicked as I am."

"Then why did he send his men to stop us?" she demanded.

"Ah, because your simple ex-husband is not privy to all of my plans, Emira Jewel. He thought you posed an actual threat, which couldn't have been further from the truth. But I trusted our wily king here to get you here safely, and he did just that."

"So what now?" I asked. So far, the ifrit Morabec gave no indication that we had turned the tables on him. Perhaps the lasso did work on djinns after all.

"Now the real fun begins," said Zeyn.

And as he motioned for his guards, I sprang forward, removing the dagger hidden inside my belt. Still holding the rope, I grabbed Morabec around the neck and held him fast.

"Go, Jewel. Now!" I pointed to the dark window high above. "There, up there!" She needed little prodding. Within moments she had removed the magic carpet.

"What is this?" bellowed Zeyn, rising to his trunk-like legs.

"This," I said, "is when the fun begins."

CHAPTER TWELVE

I stood there holding my knife to Morabec's throat, though that was mostly for show; it was the lariat loop that really pacified him. We watched as Jewel spread out the magic carpet, sat on it, and took off.

"Catch her!" Prince Zeyn shouted.

Guards converged on her, but Jewel, already airborne, sailed up out of their reach, barely eluding them. Barely was truly the word, because her skirt was flying up about her waist as the air caught it, exposing her lifted knees and thighs. Her shirt had somehow fallen open again, too, providing flashes of her breasts. That was when I realized that none of that exposure was accidental. She wanted all eyes to be locked on her instead of on me. She was giving me my best chance to solidify and escape.

The guards virtually froze in place, staring up at the parts of her that showed beyond the edges of the carpet. Even Zeyn was silent a moment, taking in that glorious scene. Jewel's thighs flexed as her feet braced against the carpet, and her breasts shook with every dip and swoop as she spiraled ever higher. Her hair was loose and whipping about her head like a living thing. She certainly knew how to hold male attention.

Meanwhile I worked the loop off Morabec, one-handed. It was complicated, because we had concealed it under his clothing.

Zeyn finally shook off his stasis. "Shoot her down, idiots!" he bawled.

Several archers lifted their bows, nocked arrows, and reluctantly aimed. It was evident they did not want to kill such a gorgeous creature.

"She won't be any good to you as a hostage or sex slave if you kill her!" I cried.

"That's right," Zeyn said. "Put the trackers on her while we fetch carpets."

Trackers? What were they?

Meanwhile Jewel passed the chandelier, reached the ceiling and flew toward the high window the little dragons used. They oriented on her, but she waved a knife and that seemed to cow them.

Then a picture formed in the center of the chamber, below Jewel. It showed her on the carpet, her evocative parts flashing, but not as seen from below. It was as if the beholder was right up there beside her.

The dragons! This was what they were seeing. Somehow they could broadcast it as a three dimensional picture the rest of us could see. They were the trackers, the spy eyes. Many eyes, gazing from all around, so that every detail could be covered. One was evidently flying in front of her, looking back, seeing right up between her lifted legs.

I couldn't blame the others for being mesmerized. At any other time I would have been too. But my life was at stake, so I allowed myself only the briefest glimpses as I continued to work on the lariat.

Jewel shot through the window and out of the castle. She could no longer be seen directly, but the spy picture continued as the dragons outside focused. We saw her emerge from the dome and make a broad circle around the fortress, still climbing. The dragons were following closely, but not attacking. This was their true purpose: to spy anything Zeyn needed to know about, whether it be an enemy formation or a lady washing in her boudoir. It was surely a significant asset in any undertaking.

Now that the direct view of the luscious creature was no longer available, men began to recover some individual purpose. Several were wrestling a large carpet out of a storage closet. That would be the pursuit craft, surely much faster than our little carpet. I had to stop that.

I wrenched the rope the rest of the way off Morabec. I leaped toward Zeyn. That was likely the last thing he thought I would do, instead of trying to flee. As his mouth opened to give an order, I used both hands to put the loop over his head and draw it snug about his shoulders. "Shut your mouth!" I whispered.

Captured and obedient, he shut it.

Now I had him. What was I to do with him? I cudgeled my lagging brain, but it seemed not to have completely caught up with events. I had no better plan than to stall, to give Jewel freedom and time to accomplish her purpose.

The men laid out the large carpet, and three got on it. They paused, awaiting further orders.

"Tell them to hold off," I murmured in Zeyn's ear. "To wait to see what the wench does."

"Follow her, but don't arrest her," Zeyn said. "Wait and see what she's up to."

The men nodded. The carpet rose smoothly, flying up toward the window. Had I succeeded in giving Jewel enough time to reach the turret and fetch the ifrit?

"Now make it seem that you are interviewing me," I said. "Allow no interruption while we talk."

"Leave us while I question this cur," Zeyn snapped.

The guards obeyed. Soon we were alone in the chamber.

Now what? "Why do you want to conquer the mortal realm?" I asked Zeyn. I just wanted to get him talking to see what I could learn, while Jewel got Lamprey and made her escape.

"Because it's there, idiot," he snapped. "Why should I settle for local power, when I can have more?"

This was not quite as submissive as I had hoped. "And you went to all that trouble to capture the Ifrit of the Lamp, just to get at me? Isn't that like using a catapult to blast a gnat?"

"Ask not about what concerns you not, lest you learn what pleases you not."

That was surely good advice, but there was something about his attitude that annoyed me. So I persisted. "What aren't you telling me?"

"That would take years to clarify, you ignorant has-been. What do you want first?"

For some reason I remained dissatisfied. Either the lariat was not working on him, and he was stringing me along, or he was telling the truth. I considered the first prospect. Why would he pretend to be subject to my will, instead of simply summoning his men and making me truly prisoner on the spot?

Maybe because he was stalling for time, just as I was. But why? What possible advantage could he gain by faking captivity, whether for a minute or a year? When he already had me where he wanted me? What else could he want?

Jewel. She had shown herself to be a lovely and feisty woman, the kind any prince would love to capture and subdue. To bind and rape repeatedly while she screamed, until at last she lost her will to fight and accepted him. At which point he might throw her away, because it was her fighting spirit he desired as much as her body. But if he tried too soon, she might throw herself off the carpet and plunge to her death, rather than submit. He needed to give her time to get to a safe place. A place where he could fetch her without risking her death.

If on the other hand the lariat was working, he might be trying to fend me off with complexities, until his men caught on and rescued him. I needed to get at the relevant truth before that happened. So maybe it did not make much difference whether the lariat was working or he was faking it; he would give me similar answers.

"Jewel," I said. "The woman. What does she need to know, that she doesn't?"

Zeyn eyed me with what might just possibly be a faint smattering of dawning respect. "She's flying into a trap."

I didn't like this at all. "What trap?" I could see in the animated picture, that was still running, that Jewel had not yet entered the tower. She was trying to pry a bar off the small window so she could squeeze in.

"She's going for Ifrit Iften, right? In the topmost turret? Morabec may have omitted a detail about that."

"What is it?"

"Iften is there; Morabec was unable to lie to you. But neither did he have to tell you the whole truth, unless you asked for it. Iften is guarded by the Queen."

He was delivering it in bits and pieces. I had to keep zeroing in on the essence. "Your wife?"

Zeyn laughed thunderously. "Some wife! No, she's Queen of the Hive. Quite fetching when she chooses to be; she has surely been giving Iften the romancing of his life. But she is not human. She merely assumes that form when it is convenient for her. When she gets serious, she reverts to her real form, complete with what you might think of as a stinger."

I quailed inside. I had heard of this type of giant insect. "What has this to do with Jewel?"

"Well, the Queen can fornicate with a male only so long before she has to plant her eggs. For that she needs another female, species largely irrelevant. You have seen fit to deliver such a female to her."

"Jewel!" I said in anguish.

"The same. I would really have liked to have taken her for myself, but this is better. Or worse, from your perspective. Our local women all know about the Queen, and will kill themselves rather than get near her. That's another reason we keep her isolated, though if she managed to break out of the tower cell she would readily fly away and leave us alone. She doesn't really like being captive, oddly."

"What's going to happen to Jewel?" Aladdin asked grimly.

"I thought you'd never ask! She will squeeze through the bars of the window and come to Iften. Whereupon the sultry woman with him will take hold of her, transform to her natural state, and apply her stinger in the ravishment of all time, depositing scores of fertile eggs. Jewel will swell up like a melon, and in due course will birth all those insects, if you could call it birthing."

He was enjoying this entirely too much. "Why not call it that?"

"Because there may not be enough left of her to expel them through that channel, after they have gorged on her flesh from the inside. I understand it's as disgusting, not to mention painful, a process as a briefly-living person can suffer. Fortunately she will not annoy us with her screams; they eat out the tongue and voice box first, as delicacies."

He was probably pulling my chain. But I couldn't risk it. "We're going to spare her that."

"Oh, I doubt it, hero," he said with heavy irony. I know I wouldn't have liked him even on a good day.

Jewel had succeeded in prying one bar out, and was working on the second. She would be inside soon.

"You have another flying carpet," I said.

"What makes you think—"

"Get over to the closet and fetch it out," I ordered, marching him in that direction.

He obeyed, as he had to, one way or another. Soon we had a second large carpet laid out. I put him on it, and got on behind him. "Guide us there, fast," I said. "And know that this pressure on your fat back is the point of my dagger. If you even think of any tricks, I'll stab first and deal with the mess after. Now get us moving."

The carpet lifted smoothly and ascended to the window and out. We flew rapidly toward the topmost turret. Jewel was no longer in sight; she had finally made it into the dread chamber. I repressed a shudder.

"There is one thing you did not think to ask," Zeyn remarked. There was a satisfied smirk in his voice.

"What, lest I learn what pleases me not?"

"Exactly."

"So what is it?"

"It is this, you utter naïve fool. Prince Zeyn has been the subject of many assassination attempts, so he takes precautions. I am not Zeyn; I am a simulacrum in his image, employed to preside at boring functions. You never came close to control of him, your lariat notwithstanding." He chuckled. "Now do with me what you wish; it will not save your wench, who is surely getting royally plumbed about now."

I knew with sick certainty that he was finally telling the relevant truth.

CHAPTER THIRTEEN

Up we raced, scattering the little fire-belching dragons, who were, in fact, the eyes of the wizard.

Wherever he may be, I thought ruefully, wondering just where this vile creature was waiting and watching. But I had little time to concern myself with such matters. I thought idly of shoving the impostor off the carpet, but even I couldn't watch a man plummet to his death. If a man he be, that is. Perhaps his inherent magical talents would save him, or perhaps not. I didn't know, but for now I held on to the lariat. Perhaps the ifrit imposter would prove valuable. Or perhaps not. We would see.

For now, I continued holding in the back of my mind thoughts of levity, anything that would keep me from densifying and plummeting to the floor below.

Up we raced, as I commanded the Zeyn simulacrum to direct the magic carpet. Wind whipped my hair. I held on to a frayed edge of the carpet with one hand, riding low. Often, as we turned hard right or left, I was nearly thrown from the damn rug. Each time the ifrit grinned, and I cursed.

We shot up a flight of stone steps, lit with torches, and as we reached the landing and barreled around a right turn, I heard a blood-curdling scream.

"Faster!" I commanded.

Amazingly, the rug, surely built for speed and maneuverability, accelerated faster still. Wind screamed over my ears. Recessed doorways passed in a blur. This time I saw the left turn coming, and sensed the ifrit bracing himself. I braced, too, and we hit the turn at nearly ninety degrees. It was all I could do to hold on to the rug and not be thrown off. Indeed, if not for my sure grip, I would have been slammed into the hallway wall.

"There," said the simulacrum, pointing.

I saw it, too. An open door at the far end of the hallway. Torchlight flickered within. Shadows crawled over the walls.

"We're going through," I said grimly.

"We cannot fit!"

"Then I suggest you command the carpet to angle in."

He did so, commanding the thing with barely audible words, and almost instantly one side of the rug dropped down. We both hung from the thing as if clinging to the top of a brick wall, and we swooped into the massive chamber.

The carpet and we circled above, and what I saw below was both a relief and a pleasant surprise. What I saw was hardly worthy of such a desperate flight: two women in bed, one of whom was completely without clothing. She had long, strawberry-colored hair, a narrow waist and a full backside. The scene might have been something out of any man's fantasy if not for the ghastly stinger protruding from the full backside.

The creature had mounted Jewel, who was currently bleeding profusely from cuts to her eyes and lips. Obviously she had done her best to fight off the creature, only to have finally succumbed to its undoubtedly great strength.

"We are too late," said the ifrit with satisfaction. "She's about to be implanted. Nothing can pry her loose."

Jewel looked up and saw me. She was about to scream but held her tongue. Wise girl. As of yet, the Queen was too focused on her prey to notice us in the chamber.

"Not good enough," I said. "Surely there is some way to unmount this creature."

The ifrit shook his head, grinning from ear to ear. I hated him even more. "Sorry, hero. But once she has a female mounted, it is all but done. Look, already her stinger is preparing for insertion."

Indeed, the long, curved apparatus was veritably quivering in anticipation. The creature struggled only with parting Jewel's legs.

The emira fought valiantly; indeed, she lashed out and landed a wonderful hooking punch that rocked the Queen. Enraged, the creature bellowed and began transforming before our very eyes into something that resembled a great hornet.

Jewel screamed and I didn't blame her.

But I also saw my opportunity.

As the creature metamorphosed, its body elongating and taking on a horrific shape, it sat back slightly, releasing some of its weight.

"Go to her now," I commanded. "And when we reach her you are to take her place."

"Please, no!" But even as he begged me, the carpet shot down from the high ceiling, racing toward the great bed.

I held on grimly, bracing myself, saying nothing. I had been a ruler once. I had been forced to hand down harsh sentences. This ifrit who relished Jewel's misery was no friend of mine. He was an enemy of the highest order.

He continued to beg and plead but I ignored his cries for mercy. There was no mercy here, not in this vile place. And not by me.

The creature was nearly metamorphosed, its smooth, elongated head the last to transform. Most important, some of its weight was off Jewel.

She saw us coming, and just as the giant insect was about to position itself on her again, she held up her hand and I grabbed it. And just as I commanded, the ifrit, very much against his will, leaped from the carpet. What happened next couldn't have been better rehearsed if we tried. I pulled Jewel up onto the carpet, even while the simulacrum took her place. And as I released the rope, thus releasing my connection to him, he tried desperately to crawl away. Too late. The stinger came down viciously...and deeply. He cried out, cursing my name, but already Jewel and I were gaining some altitude.

"Lamprey!" shouted Jewel in my ear. She pointed to an ornate bureau in the far corner. "He's already inside. I freed him just prior to that....that *thing* appearing."

That *thing* bellowed in rage, having just now noticed it had been duped. It spun around, drawing out its stinger from deep within the simulacrum, who had reverted back to his original form—that of a balding, middle-aged man. He was quite dead. Apparently the creature's stinger, which also acted as an egg depositor, killed males, while undoubtedly keeping females alive. Magic at its most deadliest. I felt nothing for the ifrit who, likewise, had felt nothing for Jewel's own dire predicament.

The queen, easily twice my own size, flapped her wings impossibly fast and rose from the bed. I was still high above it, circling around to the lamp. The creature rose straight up, watching me closely, turning with me. Its thorax flexed and it brought up its great stinger, presently covered in a dark liquid—the ifrit's blood, I assumed. The beast, I saw, could fly forward and sting at the same time.

Now we were over the lamp and I dove down, commanding the carpet with voice prompts and slight adjustments of the rug itself. Surely, there was a smoother way to fly these things, but I would have to make do.

The bureau approached rapidly. Too rapidly, I was going to crash. Jewel reached a calm hand, adjusted the carpet, stated her own command, and the magical contraption altered course. Unfortunately, so did the giant hornet above, which was now bearing down on us.

"Grab it!" she shouted.

And I did, swooping the polished lamp off the bureau, and ducking as the giant stinger swooshed over my head.

Merciful Allah, but that was close!

"Just hang on!" shouted Jewel. "I have a score to settle with this oversized dung beetle!"

And hang on I did. Jewel had proven herself to be much more adept at maneuvering the flying carpet, which was just as well. It was all I could to hang on to the lamp and the carpet at the same time.

We whipped out of the chamber and down the long hall. The demon hornet gave chase, proving to be just as mobile as the carpet, if not more so. And, apparently, faster.

It was gaining on us, buzzing down the hallway.

Jewel looked back once, and actually grinned. "Hold on tight, your highness," she said, her words heavy with sarcasm, especially the last one.

Although we sat side by side, Jewel was positioned more in the middle, her arms spread wide, her hands gripping the carpet's forward corners. Myself, I held only one lonely edge and sat low, cradling the lamp as best as I could, praying to Allah to spare me this one last time.

"You're dragging us down, imbecile!" she shouted.

Indeed, my simple prayer had occupied that part of my mind previously reserved for thinking light thoughts. I quickly filled my thoughts with images of clouds and feathers and women's undergarments, and soon we were picking up speed again. Jewel shook her head without comment.

"Get ready," she said.

And now we plunged down the winding stairs, going round and round blindly, heedless of anyone or anything that might be in our way. I nearly closed my eyes. Nearly. Except heroes didn't close their eyes. And a good thing, too.

"Look out!" I shouted.

She saw it, too, and not a moment too soon. An archway had appeared in our flightpath. I densified and she angled down and we just narrowly avoided disaster. We swept out the same upper story window and out into the throne room. I looked back. The demon hornet easily avoided the archway and burst out of the window like a cannon shot. It quickly gained on us.

The throne room, remarkably, was much different than when I had last seen it. The guards were nowhere to be found. Surely they would have returned by now after being dismissed earlier by the simulacrum, but no. The hallway so empty and quiet that I knew immediately something was wrong.

But there was no time to worry about that. The hornet was gaining. Jewel shouted a warning to me, and then turned hard, banking to port. We slewed through the air, briefly out of control, and then regained our magical traction again. The hornet made the turn easily and I was beginning to think it was only a matter of time—perhaps seconds—before the monster was upon us.

And I knew immediately what I had to do. It was me, of course, who was weighing us down. Me and my flighty thoughts of levity. I pointed to a far wall, where a great sword hung, crossed with another.

"Drop me off there!" I shouted, pointing to the floor beneath the swords.

Jewel looked at me slantwise, but did not question me. She knew I was the dead weight slowing us down. She leaned forward and we angled down. Behind us the flying beast angled with us. Its humming drone was louder as it got closer and closer. It didn't sound happy.

The wall was upon us and if Jewel didn't do something now, we were going to crash into it.

"Uh, Jewel."

"Hang on!"

As the wall rose up before us, she threw her weight hard to the right, yanking her arms with her, and the carpet came to a nearly abrupt halt. I was dislodged immediately, tumbling head over tail, slamming hard into the wall.

She looked down at me, grinning. "I told you to hang on, your highness."

The hornet was coming in fast and I urged her to go and she did so, snapping the carpet and giving a sharp order. She sped off as the flying creature banked hard, turning and following.

I next watched an aerial display the likes of which I had never seen before, nor would I expect to see again. With the extra weight off the carpet, woman and beast were nearly evenly matched. When Jewel looped, so did the creature. When she turned hard to starboard in ever tightening circles, the creature followed. And while they did this mid-air dance, I reached up and took hold of one of the curved scimitars, pulling it free from the wall. It was a good weapon, and felt natural in my hands

"Over here!" I shouted up to her. "Lure it over here!"

It was time to end this…and I would do this the only way I knew how, with the sword.

Jewel heard me and responded by heading directly at me. I watched her approach and fought the desire to duck, trusting her already. Indeed, at the last possible moment, she pulled up, and swung off the carpet and into my arms.

The hornet was directly behind, arching its thorax and lifting the stinger before it. It was going to impale one of us to the wall. My guess was me.

I wasn't wrong. It was coming for me, and it was coming hard.

I raised the sword before me, visualizing the stinger as nothing more than a javelin held by a charging desert warrior. And as Jewel dove to one side, I swung the scimitar with all my strength, deflecting the stinger, and the hateful creature sailed to one side. Its stinger, surely as hard as any steel, drove deep into the fortress wall.

And what happened next surprised even me.

A great bellow erupted from seemingly everywhere at once. The walls of the fortress shook. The ornate throne toppled over and the crystal chandelier from above crashed to the floor. I lost my footing and fell into Jewel. She pointed to a far wall, where a massive face had appeared over the stones. I knew the ugly face immediately. It was Prince Zeyn.

The real Prince Zeyn.

Jewel pointed to the adjoining wall, and I saw it, too. His face was there as well. In fact, his face now covered every wall in the room, including the ceiling and floor, stretching from corner to corner.

As the demon hornet struggled to free itself from the wall, I saw that the face of Prince Zeyn, along the same wall as the beast, was in great pain.

He was in pain from the hornet sting.

"Get the carpet!" I yelled.

Jewel immediately complied, fetching the rug which lay in a heap at her feet. "What's happening, my king?"

My king…those words sounded so nice coming from her, but I had little time to revel in them.

"The fortress is alive," I said, as we sat together on the carpet. It lifted immediately. All around us more fixtures fell and crashed.

"I do not understand," she cried out.

"Prince Zeyn *is* the fortress. He is everywhere at once."

"But how?"

"It's an illusion, of course. All of this. Now go, go!"

CHAPTER FOURTEEN

The carpet flew toward the main entry. But a portcullis appeared, looking an awful lot like huge teeth, and crunched down ahead of us. Had we been a trifle faster, it would have caught us and chewed us in half. As it was, we were merely trapped inside the main chamber.

"There's got to be other exits," I said.

The carpet spun about and zoomed across the room toward another entry. But this also sprouted teeth and snapped shut before we got there.

We swerved again, toward a third passage, but this too got bitten off.

"He's playing with us," Jewel said grimly.

"He wants to recapture us alive," I agreed. "That's probably bad news."

"So he can flay you a sliver at a time," she said. "And tie me down for the queen to screw."

I looked across at the queen. She had almost succeeded in pulling her stinger loose. She would be very angry when she resumed the hunt. We had little remaining time to dither. "We've got to surprise him," I said. "Do the unexpected."

"He expects us to try to escape."

"Ah, but the manner of it is what makes the difference."

"Well, get your manner moving!"

"The turret," I said. "Go back there."

"Oho!" The carpet reoriented and shot across to the passage leading to the turret stairway. The change was so sudden that the teeth there did not have sufficient time to clamp. They formed as we squeezed through, and gnashed down just behind us, snagging the rear of the carpet. It abruptly halted, and we slid off the front.

I landed on my backside, and Jewel landed on me. At any other time I would really have noticed how her plush posterior mashed my groin, her slender torso fitted itself to mine, and her lustrous hair flung out to caress my face. But unfortunately I was too busy to appreciate any such things.

"We've got to stop meeting this way," she murmured, and pried herself free.

I scrambled to my feet, grabbed the carpet, and yanked. But it remained caught on the teeth. Short of cutting it free, we couldn't free it, and I was not at all sure it would work correctly if maimed in that manner. "At least it prevents the queen from following us," I said.

"Praise Allah for small favors," she said.

"Very small favors. She will surely be let through the moment she seeks passage."

We turned and ran up the winding stairway. We were soon winded. Again, at any other time I would have noticed how Jewel's bare chest was heaving, and how her disheveled tresses gave her a certain appealing wild-woman look, and especially how her bottom flexed as she preceded me up the steps. But it seemed to be my fate to be too distracted by events to take note of passing points of interest.

"I have to rest!" she gasped.

I understood. "We can't afford this extra weight," I said, regretfully divesting myself of my scimitar.

There was a sound behind us, as of something mounting the stairs.

I lurched forward, swept Jewel up into my arms, and charged up the steps. But soon I too was too fatigued to continue.

"Will this help?" Jewel inquired. She turned her face to mine and kissed me.

"You feel lighter!"

"I'm diffusing."

Ah. That did make sense. "I had thought it was just the kiss."

"That, too," she agreed, smiling.

Recharged, I charged up two more loops of the spiraling stair. But soon even that energy gave out.

However, Jewel had had time to recover, and resumed climbing on her own. I followed, relieved of the pleasant burden of her weight. Also of much of my own weight, as I diffused myself. Both of us looked the same, but we were only half our normal density.

The ascent seemed interminable, but we made it. We burst into the highest turret chamber. There was the window with the bars bent outward from Jewel's entry. Our escape!

Except for one detail. We no longer had a flying carpet.

We gazed out across the colorful landscape. We had undensified so as to be able to interact with this realm, but now a fall to the ground from this height would squash us flat. Were we trapped after all?

"If we densify," Jewel said, "We'll drop right through the fortress and go splat below."

There was another sound behind us, suspiciously like huge insect wings flying up a steep incline. The queen must finally have gotten loose, and gotten the door teeth to let her through. Our time was getting strained.

"We can do the opposite!" I exclaimed. "Because we're mortals, we can densify beyond the ability of the natives. We can also diffuse beyond their powers. We can make ourselves so light we'll float!"

"I hardly trust this," Jewel said. But she started diffusing further. So did I. What choice did we have?

"Now you are mine," the queen said, appearing at the entry. She looked almost completely human at the moment, except for the huge stinger. She must have put away her wings, knowing we had nowhere to go.

"Go sting your own ass!" Jewel said. A stranger might have gotten the impression that she did not much like the queen.

The queen walked into the chamber, enjoying the moment. "First I'd better nullify the man, because I don't like distractions while I'm seeding a female." She turned to me, inhaling impressively. She was one amazing figure of a woman, in this form. "Aladdin, there are two ways we can do this. One is to have you make your effort to impregnate me in your human fashion, and I will merely touch you with my poison, just enough to make you passive. That way I can save you for future pleasures, until I finally tire of the novelty."

And I lacked even a scimitar to deter her. I knew she could overpower me when she tried. Her luscious form was highly deceptive. Maybe it was illusion, covering her metallicly tough carapace.

"What's the other way?" I asked. I was trying to stall for time so we could diffuse further.

"You can try to oppose me. Then I will have to sting you harder, stunning you and perhaps killing you. I fear you would not much like that."

I glanced at Jewel. Had we diffused enough? I feared we hadn't. How long would it take the queen to accommodate my, as she put it, effort? "I'll try the first way."

"Excellent." She approached me, completely ignoring Jewel. That was a signal of her certainty, surely justified.

I put my arms around her. She felt exactly like a lovely woman. I kissed her. Her lips were invitingly soft. I felt her bottom. It was superlative. Taken as a whole, she was enough to make any normal man desperately desire her.

"You will prefer it on the bed," she murmured. She disengaged and went to lie on her back on the bed. Her stinger disappeared, confirmation that her present form was illusion; she could make any part of it disappear.

I was careful not to look at Jewel. Even if I got stunned and could not escape, she could still get away. She had the lamp, which I hoped was losing density too; otherwise she would not be able to float away with it. More important, she knew exactly what I was doing: giving her time. Though it wouldn't have hurt to see her evince just a trace of jealousy.

I joined the queen on the bed.

"You will do better without your clothing," she murmured.

There was the problem. When I stripped she would see that I remained unready to make any "effort." I suspected Jewel, knowing this, was privately amused.

What could I do? I stripped.

"I see we are not quite ready," the queen said. "That should be readily handled." Indeed, she reached out to handle it. Then she frowned. "What's this?"

"I know your nature," I said. "That you aren't really the marvelous creature you appear. That you're a big ugly insect. That's a problem for me." And that was true, though hardly the whole truth.

"Nature, smature," she snapped. "You can get it up if you really want to." She kneaded vigorously.

Too vigorously. Her fingers sank into my substance. Because, of course, I had continued diffusing.

"So that's your game," she said. "Well, I have a spell that will stop that."

I lurched back to my feet. "Get out of here!" I said to Jewel, and plunged toward the window.

We both dived out and fell. But we were still diffusing. Our descent slowed, then stopped. We were floating.

Then the queen emerged from the window. She was now in her full insectoid splendor, and looked annoyed.

We had to get away. But how? We were floating like Chinese balloons, just waiting to be popped by the queen's stinger.

I saw some mist rising from a small lake beyond the fortress. "Get into that!" I called. I stroked my arms as if swimming. Gratifyingly, it worked.

Our progress was dismayingly slow compared to the queen's powered flight. But we managed to make it to the mist, which fortunately was thicker than it looked. Soon we were hidden in fog. I heard the queen zooming back and forth through it, searching for us. Our luck would not hold long.

"Now get down to the ground and densify," I called.

We densified, and that brought us to a landing on the shore of the lake. But now the mist was clearing, and I knew that all too soon the queen would see us and attack. This time there would be no miss-nice-girl foolishness about her. I'd soon be dead and Jewel would be worse off.

"Keep densifying," I said. "We have to find some bedrock to stand on."

"Why not just go underground?"

"Because the queen will be tracking us, and Zeyn will bring the heavy catapults to bear, and blast us out of the ground. We need to deal with her now."

She considered. "Are you thinking what I'm thinking?"

"To let her try to breed you, only you'll be impenetrably dense."

"A fitting finish," she said with satisfaction.

We found an outcrop of bedrock and stood on it while we rapidly gained mass.

The queen emerged from the mist and spied us. She looped about and zoomed in close. "Prepare to meet your doom!" she cried.

We both did a marvelous imitation of fear and despair, which were surprisingly easy to emulate. We tried to flee, but Jewel managed to fall, landing on her back. The queen landed beside her and didn't hesitate. She held Jewel down, oriented her stinger, and plunged it in.

"What's this?" she demanded, exactly as before, with me.

"I'm dense," Jewel explained helpfully. "You got only a little way in, and now you're trapped. I am closing around you like stone."

The queen tried to yank her stinger out, but the tip of it was indeed caught. All she succeeded in doing was to move Jewel's body a little. Jewel now weighed far more than the queen did, apart from being imperviously hard.

"Oh, are you stuck?" Jewel inquired solicitously. "Let me help you with that." Her knife appeared; somehow she had managed to keep that with her. She plunged it into the queen's belly and carved. In moments she cut out the stinger by its softer base.

The queen was mortally wounded. She rolled on the ground, bleeding black ichor. I couldn't help it; I felt slightly sorry for her. Jewel had effectively gutted her just as she did men who tried to rape her.

Jewel got to her feet, reached down to grab the dangling stinger, and yanked it out of her. She scornfully tossed it down beside the queen. Then she looked at me. "Where to, friend?"

"Now we need a new plan," I said. "Zeyn will be waiting to ambush us at the bridge to the mortal realm. We have to find another way."

"Maybe Lamprey will know of one."

"Great idea!" I took the lamp from her and rubbed it.

Lamprey emerged in the form of a cloud of smoke. "I thought you'd never call," he said gruffly. He also sounded weak. Normally he would have appeared as a bearded, healthy djinn, vaguely resembling a man, if a man had been nearly eight feet tall. The fact that Lamprey had only appeared in a half-state suggested he had been weakened considerably by Zeyn; no doubt, my djinn had endured much torture to ensure his cooperation.

"How can we get out of here without getting caught?"

"There is another route. But it's awkward and dangerous."

"We'll risk it," I said.

"You remain the foolish mortal I know."

"I don't need a lecture! Where is it?"

"It's in the catacombs beneath Zeyn's fortress. But beware: wiser men than you—and I say this with considerable euphemism—have fallen prey to their hazards. Very few ever emerge from them, and virtually none do so sane. There is, however, little danger of being permanently lost in the labyrinth, because the swimming monsters will find you and consume you."

"Swimming monsters?"

"Did I forget to say? The catacombs were flooded eons ago. You must navigate them underwater."

"Oh, great!"

"Will we be able to breathe there, in our dense form?" asked Jewel.

"Aye, lass. But you will not be able to remain dense throughout; there's a bridge you must traverse." The djinn paused. "PS, woman, thanks for rescuing me, in your fashion."

"You're welcome, I'm almost sure," Jewel said. "I'll be calling in the credit the moment we return to the mortal realm."

"To be sure."

She turned to me. "What are we waiting for?"

What, indeed. It was time for the dread catacombs.

CHAPTER FIFTEEN

We left the queen where she lay and followed Lamprey's directions to a stone portal in the woods behind the fortress. Unfortunately, Lamprey only knew of the entrance *into* the catacombs but not the way *through* them. The ultimate destination was somewhere in our own world, wherever that might be.

We had diffused enough to walk comfortably over the soft earth, knowing we were vulnerable to attack. Lamprey had assured us that he felt Zeyn would be waiting for us at the bridge to the mortal realm, as no one in their right minds would have braved the catacombs. Lamprey had emphasized the words *right minds*, before slipping back into his lamp to rest and recover from the torture he had endured at the hands of Zeyn. I knew Lamprey to be a powerful wizard in his own right. I suspected that Zeyn was just that much more powerful; at least, mighty enough to overcome Lamprey and force his cooperation. Lamprey was bound to me in all aspects, even loyalty, and it would have taken a powerful spell—or a lot of pain—to break my djinn down.

And broken down he had; after all, Zeyn had found me, and had his man convince Jewel to hire me. For that, I might just be grateful to Zeyn.

With Lamprey recovering in the lamp, we were on our own. At the portal, we pushed aside some hanging vines and moss and strange, pinkish spider webs as thick as the heaviest of threads. I did not want to meet the maker of such webs.

The passage down into the catacombs was fraught with slippery moss and more spider webs. I pushed through the sticky stuff, cursing under my breath, until Jewel reminded me to densify, as she had already done. Indeed, she was passing through the webs and over the slippery stones as if neither had existed. Smite me for an infidel!

I densified and we continued on. The stone beneath was cut straight from the bowels of the earth, and it led ever deeper down. Lamprey couldn't do much, but he did provide us with a flickering light that emerged from the lamp's opening. I held the lamp before us as we descended ever deeper.

"Why did you give up the throne?" asked Jewel.

We had been descending for some time. The tunnel had long since narrowed considerably, and had we been less dense, I suspected the air would have been quite cold. As it was, we were comfortable enough.

It was a topic I dreaded, and one I had not spoken of in many years. After all, outside of Faddy and Lamprey, no one knew my true identity.

"My wife and son were killed. Assassins. I searched long and hard for the killer or killers, but they escaped. The killings ripped my heart out. It is difficult to mourn the loss of those you love and run a kingdom."

She made sympathetic noises, and I knew she was no stranger to loss. After an acceptable period of silence had passed, she said, "Have you ever thought to consider that your family was killed to remove you from the throne."

"The killer or killers couldn't have known that."

"Perhaps not, but there was a high probability of it happening. In the least, you might have done something foolish enough to lose the throne."

"So you are saying I played right into their hands?"

"I am not saying anything, my king. I am only suggesting something that, in your grief, you might have overlooked."

A very old and very deep wound seemed to have opened all over again. I set my jaw and led the way deeper into the dark depths. Jewel was wise enough to keep any further questions she might have had to herself.

We rounded a long bend in the tunnel and stopped abruptly. The tunnel dipped down into a pool of dark water. We stood at the water's edge and considered our situation. Breathing underwater should be no different for us in our present dense state, a state that was impervious to the encompassing elements. Indeed, the surrounding world was presently nothing more than a ghostly representation of it.

I led the way forward into the water. Indeed, there was hardly a ripple. Jewel followed behind and I was pleased and relieved to see that the water had no effect on the lamp, which had densified right along with us, perhaps because we were holding it. Strange magic indeed in this world, but it did make some semblance of sense. It was an odd sight holding a flickering flame under water, one that I would not soon forget.

The water itself might as well have not been there at all. Less dense than the ground we had covered upon first entering Djinnland, the water offered no resistance.

We continued along the tunnel floor, which had widened considerably. The surface was now far above and we came upon glowing little fish with scaly wings. They saw us and darted away, flapping their wings. I could only wonder when we would meet the swimming monsters.

I did not have to wait long. One such creature appeared from the murky depths, a long sinewy, snake-like creature with the head and mane of a lion. It saw us and growled ferociously, its mouth opening impossibly wide.

We had no weapons, but I knew that in our current high-dense state, a creature of lesser density should pass through us, as the worms had done earlier.

Mercifully, I wasn't wrong. Longer than a team of horses, the creature's huge jaws snapped down on us...and through us. I shuddered and the sensation and the creature seemed perplexed as well. It tried again and again, and each time the result was the same.

Finally, it regarded us, lifting its great head. "You are not from this world," it said, its voice deep, reverberating off the tunnel walls.

"What gave you that impression, devil fish?" snapped Jewel. Boy, she did not suffer fools lightly, even if they were fifty creatures of nightmares.

It glanced at her, rolling eyes as big as my head. "No matter. You will need to de-densify soon. And when you do, you will be mine. I merely have to wait. That is, of course, if you ever find the exit. Probably you won't. In that case, I will have to wait longer for you to go mad, but either way, you will eventually de-densify and I will have myself a nice meal or two."

The creature's knowledge of our situation was shocking, until I realized we were surely not the first outsiders it had seen. Like the Queen, its knowledge of our language was another matter, entirely. I suspected, perhaps, that Djinnland was imbued with a magic that permitted many of the creatures to communicate.

Or not. Perhaps I was simply mad.

It was disconcerting at best to continue along and have such a monstrous creature follow in our wake. The beast seemed patient, and that would surely be our downfall. And as we took turn after turn in the maze-like tunnels, often ending up in places I was certain we had seen before, the creature simply chuckled behind us.

This continued for some time. We resorted to marking the tunnel walls, digging our nails deep into the stone, and often we came upon the same marking. In our high dense state we also grew fatigued much faster. We sat on a ledge and looked out into the depths and a deep sense of hopelessness settled over me. Jewel, too, because she reached out and took my hand and rested her head on my shoulder, and I wondered idly what it would feel like to be bitten in half or even swallowed whole.

And as we sat there quietly, I heard something curiously coming from the lionserpent. A slight whimper, perhaps. Sometimes, mixed with the whimper, came the sound of true agony.

"We understand that you will be killing us soon," I said. "You do not need to mock us further."

It swam a little closer, flicking its great muscular tail. "I am not mocking you, my future lunch. I am in great pain."

And now it turned its face to one side and I saw the source of his pain. A great and rusted hook projected out from its cheek. A thick cord flapped in the currents.

"A fisherman tried his luck," said the beast. "He was consumed quickly, of course, for he had not expected me to rise up from the depths. But his blasted hook has haunted me for eons."

"Perhaps the fisherman had the last laugh after all," snapped Jewel again. Oh, but I would hate to get on her wrong side!

Still, I saw an opportunity here.

"Do you know these catacombs well?" I asked.

"Know them well? I have been swimming them for countless centuries."

"And so you know the way out?"

"Of course, foolish man."

"Then I propose this: I will remove the hook from your cheek, since you have no hands. In turn you will guide us out safely and not eat us."

It shook its massive head. "No deal. I am hungry. I have lived long enough with this great pain, I can live longer still."

Jewel stepped forward. "We are but one meal, consumed quickly and forgotten. Your pain is eternal. Think on this, serpent."

"I'm not a serpent, I'm a lion."

I did not bother to argue semantics with the creature, but I saw that Jewel's words had hit home. It must have run a tongue over the inside of the hook, that part which projected into its mouth. The lion-serpent winced.

"How do you not know I will renege on our deal and eat you anyway?"

"I cannot know this," I said. "I have only your word."

"The word of a lion is sacred," it said.

"And what about the word of a serpent?" challenged Jewel.

"I am no serpent," it roared, clearly agitated. And when it was done roaring and contorting its face, it went back to whimpering like a kitten.

"You have a deal," it said. "If you remove the blasted hook from my face, I will escort you to the portal to your own land."

"And not eat us," I clarified. "No consuming us and then defecating us at the portal."

"There will be no consuming of any sort. Just please, for the love of all that which is holy, remove the blasted hook."

And so I did. With hands it was quite easy. I sucked in some air, perhaps even drawing the oxygen from the surrounding water itself, and diffused enough to grab hold of the hook. The great creature opened its great jaws and I reached inside warily and removed the heavy hook, which was as big as my arm.

When finished, the creature roared loudly and swam happily in tight circles and told us to get on. We each took in great lungfuls of air, diffused, and soon found ourselves riding high on its scaly back. Not a serpent my arse.

The creature swam powerfully through the tunnels. It also swam near the boundary, breaking the surface often, allowing us to breathe, for in our present state we were soaked to the bone and in desperate need of air.

It swam quickly, scattering flying fish before it, and soon we were in a section of the catacombs I had not seen before. It raced along, narrowly missing smooth rock walls. Jewel held on behind me, and we both rode low. Myself, I held on to the creature's thick mane.

Soon a great bridge appeared in the submerged tunnel, a ghostly shadow that spanned a depth so deep that I could not see the bottom. The lionserpent shot over this open space, and plunged back into another tunnel system, and when the creature broke the surface again, it stopped. We were in a small cavern.

"Continue along this tunnel, and you will find yourself in your own world," it said, and I could still hear the joy in its voice. To be free of pain was truly a gift, even at the price of a meal or two.

We climbed off and stood at the water's edge. The lionserpent regarded us, his magnificent head breaking the surface. From this position, it very much did look like a lion. Already, the wound in its cheek seemed to be healing.

"Thank you," I said. "For not eating us."

"Do not thank me yet, mortals. A great ogre guards the portal between worlds. And he's not as nice as me."

And with that, the lionserpent flicked its tail and disappeared.

CHAPTER SIXTEEN

We contemplated the tunnel. At least we were back on dry land, which was a relief, though we were able to handle the water. "The ogre must be a land-lubber," I said.

"I don't have much experience with ogres," Jewel said. "I'm afraid that if I tried to seduce it to get close enough for a killing thrust, it would eat me first."

"And it might be too big and tough to kill with a pinprick stab," I agreed. "But you might try flashing it from a safe distance to distract it while I try to get close enough."

"Why would an ogre have any romantic interest in my body?"

"If it's humanoid and male," I said gallantly, "it will have an interest, however unrealistic."

She glanced sidelong at me as if aware that I was speaking for myself as much as for the ogre. "You don't even have your scimitar."

She had a point. When I got naked with the queen, then floated to the ground, I lost most of my hardware. "I'll scout around for a weapon."

"As if they're going to be lying on the ground waiting for you," she said sourly.

"The prior folk the ogre has eaten—what did he do with their weaponry?"

She reconsidered. "Could be lying on the ground."

We started walking down the tunnel. Moss or lichen coated the walls, glowing faintly, which helped. In fact it was rather pretty. I reached out to touch a red flowerlike clump.

And wrenched back my stinging fingers. "Hoo!" I wailed.

Jewel had the grace not to mock my pain. "Let me see." She took my hurting hand. "Yes, that looks like an acid burn. Those flowers are not meant to be picked. At least not by the likes of us. Better rinse it off."

"And if the ogre throws us against the wall, we'll feel more than the impact," I said ruefully as I ran back to plunge my hand into the water. It helped, though I still had a burn.

We resumed walking down the tunnel. I was glad that the moss on the floor of it was not similarly acidic. Maybe that was so that victims could navigate it and reach the ogre. No point in letting him go hungry.

The tunnel opened out into a vast cave. On the far side there looked to be a gated portal. That would be our access to the mortal realm. It was about halfway up the cliff-like side, with a ramp leading to it. Not bedrock; we would have to traverse it diffused. That meant we would be ogre bait.

"Where is the ogre?" Jewel whispered.

"I suspect all we have to do to find him is venture into that cave. He's probably sleeping between meals."

"I think we need to plan our strategy before rousing him. What's your plan?"

What, indeed! Her knife was the only weapon we had, and it was surely insufficient. But she expected me to know what to do.

I cudgeled my weary brain again. It surprised me by coming up with an idea. "That acid flower—that's how the plant protects itself from being eaten by the ogre."

She didn't actually say "Duh," but it was in her look. "And your point is?"

"If we could spread that acid on our bodies, we would become inedible."

Jewel merely looked at me. She was right: the acid would kill us before the ogre did. As bright ideas went, it was a dullard.

But I thought I had hold of something that might somehow manage to work its way into a usable notion, if I gave it sufficient leeway.

"Suppose there's something we could put moss on? Without actually touching the moss ourselves? We could stab the ogre with that."

"That's better than nothing," she agreed. "Not much better, but better."

I looked around the giant cave. On a ledge nearby I saw a huge pile of bones and metal. That would be the refuse left by the ogre, tossed out of the way so he wouldn't trip on it. There might be something useful there. But I knew if I went for it, the ogre would appear and grab me.

"Jewel, I hate to ask this of you, but—"

"Got it," she said. "I'll distract him while you fish for a spear. Assuming he is humanoid and male."

"Yes, if you can safely do it."

"That alcove I think should be out of his reach." She gestured to an opening in the wall that led into a series of lesser caves. "I'll pose there, and retreat as necessary."

"Great!" I got down behind a boulder.

Jewel climbed up to the opening, checked out its recesses, then stood on the ledge overlooking the main cave. "Hey, snothead!" she called loudly. "Take a look at this." She struck a pose that made me wish yet again that a) I had my manhood back, and b) she was willing.

There was a deep growl from the recesses. The ogre was stirring. Or was it an earthquake? The very floor of the cave was rising, giving off steam.

It was indeed the ogre. I had thought he would be typical of the breed, meaning twice a man's height and, if an erstwhile court math man was to be believed, eight times a man's mass. But this monster was bigger than that. His shaggy head alone seemed to be as tall as a man, and every ivory garbage-stained tooth a six inch dagger.

Stab him to death? Any spear I might wield would be no more than a toothpick!

"Take a look at me, poop brain," Jewel blithely continued. She still thought I could find something to take out this behemoth?

The ogre's great dull eyes blinked. I thought I almost heard a clang as the upper lids struck the base lids. He sat up and leaned toward her. He was so big that he could readily reach her sitting. His skin hung in armored folds like those of an African rhino I had seen once. His eyes seemed not to see at all well, but still well enough to place us, and probably he heard better than that. So he knew where we were.

Nevertheless, I got moving while the ogre wasn't peering my way, and made it to the pile of refuse. It was a tangled mess, and it stank of not-quite-completely rotted flesh. But I did find a pike in it, significantly longer than I was and stoutly made, tapering to a point. Would that do it?

I looked back at the ogre. Who was I fooling? Assuming I could even maneuver the thing and thrust the pike at him, I would lack the power to dent his horny skin.

I delved further, and discovered a straight sword, the kind the barbarian Crusaders used. Clumsy thing, adorned with the infidel cross. Served the dope right to get eaten. But maybe this crude instrument would do. I pulled it out, admiring its rusty length.

"What do you think of this, vomit head?" Jewel asked the ogre. She was striking another pose, showing her torso off to such advantage that I had to avert my gaze lest I be stunned. The ogre put his disreputable puss close to get a better view, and I saw that his gross dirty eyeball was knee-high on her. At least he seemed to appreciate pulchritude when it was right in his ignorant face.

Meanwhile I took the sword and retreated to the mossy wall behind it. I pushed the sword into the brightest moss flowers I found, and saw the acid practically squirting onto the blade. With luck, the dirt and rust would hold more of it there.

Holding the dripping weapon out well away from my body, I made my way slowly back toward Jewel, who continued to distract the ogre. I saw the monster's enormous tongue come out and slurp across his washboard lips. Was he thinking of sex—or food? I suspected the latter. One grab, and he would have his morsel. He would squish her into pulp, then lick up the juice.

And I got a wild idea. If the ogre wanted to grab, let him grab!

"Jewel!" I called. "Diffuse!"

The monster's head turned slowly toward me, registering a second morsel. Did he understand me? I doubted it, but I didn't care. I had the way to take out the monster. If it worked.

"So the thing can't touch me?" she called back.

"Something like that."

"But we won't be able to push the portal gate open if we're diffuse."

"Don't worry about it."

Meanwhile I started densifying. I held on to the sword, taking it with me, or at least the hilt. I remained amazed by the ambition of my idea.

In due course Jewel joined me behind the boulder. She had diffused, and I had densified, so that when we touched our hands passed right through each other almost without resistance. "You're not diffuse!" she exclaimed.

"Pay close attention," I said. "I have soaked this old sword in moss-flower acid. It should really sting Ogre-face if I can get close enough to strike a vulnerable part."

"And make him mad enough to squish us both against the wall like paste," she said.

"Maybe not. I think he understands you when you talk. Maybe not perfectly, but he listened and looked."

"I should hope so, considering the show I put on."

"It was some show," I agreed. "But now I want you to put on another show. I want you to emulate the queen, with her stinger."

"Maybe if I had a real stinger, that would make sense. But the ogre won't fall for a fake one. He'll just grab and squish and chomp."

"Exactly.

"I'll be dead!" she said severely.

"No. Not in your diffuse state. The ogre can't touch you, literally."

"And I can't touch him. But that won't take him out."

"This will take him out," I said, indicating the sword. "Once I get close enough to use it."

"On that rhino hide? I am not following your reasoning."

I clarified my reasoning. Her doubt converted to amazement. "That just might work!"

"It had better."

"You have a mind like an insane genius."

"Thank you."

She kissed me on the forehead. Unfortunately I couldn't feel it; she was cloud-like, while I was totally dense.

We organized and rehearsed, choreographing our words and motions. This had to be done right, or it would leave us unable to escape this realm. We had to escape, because Zeyn was surely searching for us with rape and torture on his evil mind.

When we were as ready as we could be, we did it. I stood up, and Jewel stood. Then she stepped into me. Our naked bodies overlapped, so that the two of us stood in the same place. It looked as if she were holding the sword, and as if I had breasts. What I wouldn't have given to have tried to overlap her like this when we both were the same density! It might even have cured my impotence.

Then we stepped out from the cover of the boulder. "Hey feces face!" Jewel called. "I am going to drive you out of this cave!"

The gigantic shaggy head rotated so the tub-sized eyes could orient balefully on her.

"Know why? Because I'm the insect queen. See my stinger!" She raised her arm, and I raised mine with it, so that the sword seemed to be in her hand. "Mess with me, and I'll sting you so hard you'll cry like a baby! Got that, bone butt?"

The ogre grimaced. Yes, he understood enough.

We stepped carefully out toward the exit ramp. It was important that the ogre make his move before we got there, because in our present state we couldn't use it. Jewel would float through it, and I would densify through it, giving us away.

The cunning brute waited until we were too far clear of the boulder to run for cover. Then he swept his monstrous horny hand down to grab. Good!

His hamfingers closed around our body. They didn't actually touch it, because of our densities, but just at the right time I jammed the tainted sword into the soft pad of his thumb. I hoped the tip remained close to normal density, and the acid with it. This was the acid test.

The ogre paused. A look of slow bewilderment labored to cross his dull puss. Then at last he got the message. “OOOOOWWOOO!!” he howled, yanking back his limb.

“I warned you, sick sack,” Jewel said. “I stung your filthy paw. One dose probably won’t kill you, because of your size, but I’ve got more where that came from. Want to try for another?” She lifted her arm high, and I followed, waving the sword.

The ogre considered for about fifteen seconds as his dull brain processed the invitation and its significance. Then he drew back farther and stuck his thumb in his mouth. Naturally that spread the acid to his tongue. After another fifteen seconds he caught on, spat out the thumb, and lumbered away, howling.

“You big baby!” Jewel called after him gleefully.

“We may not have much time,” I said. “You densify. I’ll diffuse. Then we’ll run up the ramp and out.”

“I’ll thicken, you thin,” she agreed. “But put that sword down before we get high on acid.”

Good point. I set down the infidel sword. It had served its purpose.

I started feeling odd. Then I realized that we were still overlapping. We were feeling each other’s bodies, and not in the normal sense. “I hate to say this, but I think we’d better separate, at least by enough to give us each our own space.”

“True. I don’t think I’d look good with a penis.” She half smiled. “Not a flaccid one, anyway.” She stepped out of me and stood gloriously separate.

“Or I with breasts,” I agreed. “Even such splendid ones as yours.”

We approached normal density and started up the ramp. Jewel still tended to float, and I tended to wade, but we were zeroing in on the proper range.

Now we saw that the portal was barred by a portcullis far too massive for us to move. We could not squeeze between the bars. We would have to change densities again to get by it.

Then the ogre returned. He must have realized that he was leaving perfectly good meat behind. This time he carried a wad of cloth to shield his hand from stings. He wasn’t totally stupid.

"Hurry!" Jewel said.

We ran up the rest of the ramp, gaining speed as we adjusted to its density. We reached the portal just as the ogre swung his hamfist at us. We threw ourselves to the sides as that massive club crashed into the portal gate.

And shoved it out of the way. The brute had unwittingly freed us.

He drew back his hand for another pass. We scrambled through and into a widening cave.

We were free. Maybe.

CHAPTER SEVENTEEN

The cave turned into another tunnel, and at the far end of the tunnel we could see bright light. Glorious bright light.

We picked up our pace, wary for any other subterranean creatures, but, alas, the ogre was the last of them.

Shortly, the tunnel opened onto a sheer cliff. I pulled up short, gasping, and reaching back to stop Jewel from bumping into me, although, normally, such contact wouldn't have been a bad thing. In this case, it could have been fatal.

"What is it?" she asked, and stepped cautiously next to me.

We both stood at the tunnel's end, looking down into a misty void. What lay below was most certainly death, or something close to it. What lay before us was only hinted at: the broken remnants of a destroyed bridge. Unfortunately, between us and the end of the broken bridge was about fifty feet of nothing.

No, not quite nothing. Something screeched from below. I looked down, and up from the mist rose a spectacular winged creature, rising so quickly that I would have had my head bitten off by its long, scissor-like beak if not for Jewel yanking me back into the tunnel. The beast rushed past the cave opening in a blur of red and gold feathers, its bony beak snapping. Wind thundered over us, created by the creature's powerful downdraft. If there was anything positive about facing a massive and horrific winged creature, it was that it was too massive for the cave itself. Instead, we caught glimpses of it circling outside, emerging in and out of view, and in and out of the swirling mist.

"By Alla, someone doesn't want us to leave," I said.

"Which is why Zeyn never expected us to take this route. And if we were foolish enough to do so, he would assume we could never survive."

Seeing what lay before us, I was beginning to see the folly in this plan. Still, we were too far now to go back.

"What do you suggest?" I asked.

"Perhaps the winged creature has a hook in its beak, as well."

I looked sideways at Jewel and saw the small smirk on her face. I reached out and took her by the waist and pulled her toward me. She went willingly. "You pick a fine time to jest."

"And you pick a fine time to hold me close," she countered, and she lay a long-fingered hand over my forearm. Her touch was blessedly warm and comforting.

We looked at each other for a long moment. Perhaps if we were in our mortal realm, we would have felt the pressure to find and save her son in time, but here, in Djinnland, we were out of time, so to speak.

And as her hand slid up my forearm, I was struck with an idea.

"We are still in Djinnland!" I said. Indeed, I could sense my heightened form weighing down on my knees and lower back.

She nodded. "No one ever said King Aladdin was a fool."

"No, I mean, yes, but if we are Djinnland we can still diffuse."

She narrowed her eyes, and then they widened again. "And perhaps diffuse so much that we float out over the gorge, safe from falling and the winged creature."

"It is worth a try," I said.

Her smile told me that I was onto something. And now she made her slowly moving hand reach up to the back of my head where her fingers ran through my hair. She pulled me in close with surprising strength and our mouths met in a deep and satisfying kiss.

When she pulled away, I was left gasping and mildly aroused. In fact, more than mildly. By Allah, there was hope for me yet. Jewel seemed to sense what she had done; indeed, she had no doubt *felt* what she had done. She smiled impishly.

"Shall we diffuse, my king?"

"After that kiss," I said, shaking my head and tucking Lamprey's lamp in my belt. "I shall have to work thrice as hard to diffuse now."

She giggled and we spent the next few minutes focusing our thoughts on all things light and weightless. I found that my idiot thoughts were focused on Jewel and her body and her lips, and I saw that I was lagging behind. Jewel was already so diffused that I could see through her. Indeed, she veritably floated before me.

"Now, now, Niddala," she said playfully. "Focus."

And so I did. I tore my eyes away from her and focused on what had prompted me to diffuse back when we had first entered Djinnland: the mist. Soon, I felt my body lighten.

"More," said Jewel. "Keep going."

I watched the mist swirl and churn, doing my best to ignore the flying beast. I wondered what it would be like to be mist, to be free of a heavy mass entirely. Such freedom, indeed.

"Good, good. More."

I saw myself as mist. I saw myself as nothing, in fact, and soon I felt unburdened completely. Soon I felt as light as the air itself.

"You have done it, my king. Shall we go?"

I led the way trepidly. But floating a few inches above a tunnel floor was a far cry different than floating above a bottomless canyon. To propel ourselves we made swimming motions with our arms and legs, and quickly we were out over the swirling mist. The great winged creature, who had been flying above us, saw us, spotted us, even in our diffused state, and tucked its wings in and dove down.

"Hang on," I said.

"To what?"

Its long, snapping beak passed through us, just as the lionserpent's jaws had. The sensation was an odd one at best, one that sent a shiver through me.

We continued flying while the great raptor continued attacking. It was all I could do to hold my thoughts on all things light, while swimming over certain death and with a blasted devil bird snapping its beak through me.

But we managed, and none too soon.

As the broken edge of the bridge drew closer, I felt myself densifying naturally. I was returning to my natural state in the mortal realm.

"Hurry!" I urged, swimming rapidly.

It was truly a race to the edge of the bridge before we had solidified so much that we no longer remained afloat. And the denser we became, the more we were prone to the creature's attacks.

I felt myself dropping. Jewel dropped, as well, but not as much. I was heavier and denser naturally. I swam hard, pulling at the air with my hands, willing myself forward.

I heard thunderous flapping behind me. The creature was bearing down on me, on us. Surely we would soon be dense enough to be vulnerable.

We swam. The raptor flapped. The broken edge of the bridge appeared before us—

Jewel made it, alighting smoothly on the damaged edge, but I didn't. Not quite.

As I dropped, as I felt my stomach rise up to the back of my throat, I reached out and just managed to grab the crumbling edge of the broken bridge.

"Look out!" screamed Jewel above me.

I raised my legs just as something massive and powerful swept below me, brushing past me so hard that I nearly lost my grip. The beast's great beak and snapped shut so hard that it sounded as if its bony jaws had shattered. It screeched angrily below, banking to port and making its way back toward me.

A hand reached down from above. Jewel's hand. Was she strong enough to hold me? I didn't know, but I also didn't have enough time to debate. I grabbed her hand and she pulled. I swung my legs up and over the shattered section of bridge.

We both flattened ourselves as the great bird passed overhead, and then we were running as fast as we could, through the broiling mist that hung over the bridge and to the mortal realm.

CHAPTER EIGHTEEN

Suddenly the mist abated. We were emerging from a cave in the side of a mountain. Familiar trees and grass grew on the rocky hillside. We were back in the mortal realm!

I turned around to make sure there was no pursuit. But I saw nothing. We were on a vague little path that twisted up the mountain with no sign of any cave.

We both threw ourselves down and kissed the blessed turf. Then we sat up and kissed each other. She was soft and sweet and wholly divine.

"Do I take this to mean—" I started.

"Not until after you rescue my son."

Oh. Yes. Of course. She was merely motivating me with the hint of how she could be once I completed my end of the deal. "After," I agreed.

"But you know, when you return to your rightful place on the throne, you may not find me so interesting. I am no longer young, and I am well used. I gutted my rapists, but the damage was done."

So it had been rape, not seduction. That made a difference. "I'm not interested in returning."

"You have to return. You were a fair to middling king, but much better than what's likely to take your place. King Huran, whom you appointed, lacks verve. He won't last much longer."

"I'd rather be with you."

"You're too foolishly romantic. What would it take to persuade you?"

"You as my queen. With your guidance I might well be more than a fair to middling king."

That set her back. "That's a steep price. I thought all you wanted was your manhood back."

"That, too," I agreed. "Originally."

"Save my son, and I'll give you that. In fact I'll be your concubine, if you want. But I'm wary of marriage."

Well, that was half a loaf. Best not to push too far, lest I lose my gains. "You have reason." I looked around. "I'm not sure where we are, but it looks familiar."

"The other side of Abu Bakr's property."

"You must have an excellent awareness of terrain!"

"Thank you."

"We'd better get down to see him. Then—"

"Then on to Samarkand. We're back in real time now, and that's limited."

"Yes. Let me check with Lamprey as we walk." I set off down the path, and Jewel paced me. Maybe with luck there'd be narrow places, so I could do the gallant thing and let her precede me, and I could appreciate her backside in motion.

"Check first with Faddy. He's a better companion." An obscure expression crossed her features. "Compliment him. I think he can do more for you than he has before, if so inclined."

"He's an ifrit. He obeys my directives."

That obscure expression still hovered close. "Ifrits may be a bit like women. They perform better when treated like people."

What did she mean by that? "Why?"

"Even an animal does better when granted a modicum of respect and encouragement. Think of your experience with horses."

Now she was making sense. A well trained, well treated horse was a vital asset. I rubbed my ring.

Faddy appeared, floating to my other side. He was no longer invisible, as he knew I was no longer concealing him from Jewel. He was a halfway handsome figure of a middle-aged male, with an ugly turban. "Thank you for a nice visit home, master."

"You're welcome. Your messages helped."

"You understand that they were watching me."

"Yes." Then, heeding Jewel's suggestion, I larded it on. "You behaved in a loyal, sensible manner."

Faddy paused. I could tell he was significantly pleased. "Do you need me any more, now that you have recovered the Ifrit Iften?"

"I'll always need you. You're great company. Do you have any advice?"

Faddy glanced at Jewel. "You're civilizing him already."

"Civilized men are easier to handle," Jewel said.

The ifrit's lips quirked. "In contrast to civilized women."

"Someone needs to do the handling."

"Just so." Faddy looked at me. "Iften's depleted from the savaging by Prince Zeyn. He can still do a lot more than I can, but you should probably save him for when you really need him."

That was surely good advice. I had figured on simply having Lamprey pop us to Samarkand, but chances were I needed his power also to deal with Jewel's brute of a husband. No sense wasting him on small stuff. Jewel was right to have me encourage Faddy. "But we have to get to Samarkand swiftly. He can take us there."

"But you can make it easier on him if you manage correctly."

"How so?"

"Get in the lamp."

I stared at him. "Come again?"

"Use it as a convenient transport vehicle. It will be much easier for Iften to carry the lamp there than two full-grown mortal people who need to be protected from extreme acceleration, atmospheric thinning, the chill of the heights, radiation, time dilation, and so on."

I had no idea what he was talking about. "We just want to pop out here and pop in there, the way ifrits do."

"But ifrits are immortal, largely impervious, and we can reconstitute our damaged substance. We can handle the rigors of rapid transit. You mortals are dangerously delicate."

This quibbling was annoying me. "And how could we ever fit in the little lamp?"

"The same way Iften does. Diffuse and compact."

"We're not ifrits! We're locked to our normal density here."

"Normally, yes. But the lamp is special. Invoke the right spell, and it will take you in."

"But I don't want to be squished into that tight little space!"

"It won't seem like that to you."

"We'll be squished together," Jewel murmured.

I reconsidered. How bad could it be, jammed in close to her? "Okay, we'll try the lamp. What else?"

"You will need a plan of attack. You will have time to work it out in the lamp, because it's like Djinnland: no time passes outside it, for you, regardless how long you remain inside."

Being squeezed up against Jewel for an indefinite period. The notion had its appeal. "What else?"

"One thing to be aware of is that the woman's evil ex-husband has magical assistance. We have seen the power of his allies. They will be aware of any magic practiced in their vicinity, and will home in on it instantly. Then you'll be finished."

"But we'll have Lamprey."

"Iften at full power could handle it, yes. But Iften depleted will simply get himself captured again, and you may be sure Zeyn will be more careful next time to see that he never gets sprung. Your available force is limited; you need to manage it carefully. Otherwise you are courting disaster."

"Excellent point," Jewel said. "We came close enough to disaster in Djinnland. We don't need any more of that."

"All right," I said impatiently to cover my nervousness. Disaster meant Jewel becoming a sex slave and me a monarch serving the nefarious purposes of Zeyn. We couldn't risk that. "Jewel and I will discuss it while we're in the lamp."

Jewel took my hand and squeezed it affirmatively. She was managing me, but I rather liked it.

We were arriving at Abu Bakr's house. Faddy faded out; he had become invisible. "Halloo!" I called.

The sage emerged, surprised to see us. "How is it you are returning from that direction? There is only the mountain there."

"We took a roundabout route." It seemed he did not know about the other access to Djinnland, or wasn't telling. Maybe he knew of it, but also knew how dangerous it was.

He took stock, visibly. "Did you accomplish your mission?"

"Yes. Now we need to move on to Samarkand. Have you any advice before we go?"

"If you visited Djinnland and returned intact, you need no further advice from me. Do you wish to have your horses back?"

"Keep them. We won't be using them."

"May I offer you some food for your journey?"

"Yes," Jewel said. "Make it to go."

"Are you sure?"

Jewel merely inhaled. The sage froze in place, momentarily stunned.

"We could also use some clothing," I said, remembering that we were naked. No wonder Jewel was impressing the man so. Even the oldest and wisest sage was not immune to that.

Soon we had modest clothing, a loaf of bread, and a jug of wine. We thanked the sage and departed afoot. If Abu Bakr was curious how we proposed to travel, he masked it well.

When we were alone and shielded from any observation, we organized for the journey. I rubbed the lamp.

Lamprey, or more properly Iften, emerged as a column of smoke that formed into his normal aspect. "What is your wish?"

"We want to take your place in the lamp and have you transport us to Samarkand," I said briskly. "Can you do that?"

"Readily, when so directed. Where in Samarkand?"

I turned to Jewel. "Where?"

"I don't know exactly. We'd better go to an inn while Faddy explores and locates my son."

"I don't have to take orders from you," Faddy said.

Jewel smiled at him. "It's that you have such ability and finesse that only you can do this job properly."

The ifrit, swayed, glanced at me. What powers of persuasion the woman had!

"We need you," I agreed.

"In that case, I'll be glad to."

"So be it," Lamprey said.

Then Jewel and I were in a pleasant room girt with soft cushions and a bed mat. A set of dice lay in a corner. In a moment I realized that the chamber was in the shape of a lamp. Lamprey must entertain himself shooting dice while confined here. I was aware of no motion; if the lamp was traveling at high velocity it did not seem to affect the interior. This was, in short, a comfortable way to travel.

Jewel settled on the bed with the bread and wine. "Care to join me?" she inquired. Her lovely thighs showed under her skirt as she raised her knees. That could not have been accidental.

I joined her. What else could I do? "What do you have in mind?" I asked cautiously, sure it wasn't romance.

"Our strategy, of course," she said as she tore off a piece of bread and offered it to me. She was still showing me how she could be when pleased. "We are not going to be able to simply walk in and claim my son. In fact any approach will alert them. They may even be using my son as a lure to bring us in for capture. That may have been their plot from the beginning."

That made unkind sense. "So what do we do?"

"That is for you to figure out, my lord."

"Jewel, by now you know me well enough to know that I'm not all that smart. You're going to have to help me."

"You're stupid like a fox in a grape yard. Now exert your native cunning."

"Jewel—"

"Oh, all right, you beggar." She moved close and kissed me. "Does that do it?"

"I meant some hint about where your son might be, and how I am to recognize him if I see him."

"You mean I wasted a kiss I didn't have to give?" she demanded severely. But then she smiled. "Here is my best hint: I told him long ago that if he were ever in a situation he did not trust, and perhaps feared for his life, to be wary of the food. They might use it to drug him, or as part of a ceremony."

"Such as a ritual sacrifice?"

"That was not in my mind at the time, but yes, now it fits perfectly. Gods of any stripe are choosy about what they accept as sacrifices. The offerings have to be healthy and eager to participate."

"Which means a good meal and the promise of life in paradise," I said. "Only a child will not know that the paradise is not in the mortal realm."

"Exactly. So I told him to demand something excruciatingly rare, such as yak's milk cheese."

"That's not that rare. Merchants bring it from the eastern mountains. Expensive, but available."

"With chocolate sauce."

"With what?"

"Chocolate sauce. The jinni fetch it from the far, far west, I understand. It is said to be fabulously tasty."

"That's rare," I agreed.

"Their sacrifice will not be valid without it."

"Assuming your son does ask for it."

"He's a smart boy."

Now my mind was percolating. "I know a cheese merchant who owes me a favor and can be trusted," I said. "He will tell them he can get chocolate in a week, for a ridiculously high price."

"They'll need it tonight."

"Precisely. Cowed by their offer of riches coupled with their threat of beheading him if he fails, he will reluctantly agree to have his eunuch deliver it before nightfall."

"But that will set them up to sacrifice my son!"

"Ah, but I will be there with my lamp."

"How can you be there when you don't even know where?" Then she paused. "That eunuch—you!"

"The same," I agreed. "I'll put the boy in the lamp, and we'll be off before they realize."

"You devious genius!" This time her kiss was enough to make any thought of being a eunuch dissipate in steamy smoke.

Then suddenly we were standing in a private courtyard. Lamprey had completed the journey to Samarkand and rubbed the lamp to bring us out.

It was time for action.

CHAPTER NINETEEN

Although it was mid-day and we were alone in the courtyard, a cold chill swept through me. I had trained myself to be wary of such chills. They were, in my experience, indication of dark magic.

"Faddy," I called, rubbing my ring.

The ifrit appeared by my side in a puff of billowing smoke that quickly solidified into a man. "Yes, master."

I rolled my eyes. "Please, for the love of Allah, stop calling me master."

"As you wish. Is that why you summoned me?"

"Of course not," I snapped. "Are we being watched?"

"I cannot know this until I have poked around."

"Then poke away."

"As you wish, master," he said, disappearing, and I not-so-silently ground my teeth.

Jewel came up next to me and rested a long-fingered hand gently on my forearm, causing a shiver of pleasure to course through me. She said, "You do realize that he's magically required to call you master?"

"He's also magically required to do my bidding."

"Then perhaps he enjoys toying with you. Remember, my lord, we need his help, which, I believe, could be considerable. So go lightly on him. After all, you are his master, as you are Lamprey's. Some things are inevitable."

Her words struck home, and I wondered if her speech had a deeper, perhaps more widespread meaning. Some things had been inevitable for me, like leading a kingdom, which I had readily given up in my grief and sorrow.

I said nothing; merely considered her words, and soon Faddy reappeared invisibly next to my ear. "There's a large contingent of men closing in on you. From what I gather, they were alerted by your sudden appearance. This city is heavily monitored by Zeyn and his forces. Very little magically can happen within Samarkand without his immediate knowledge, including my own appearances by your side."

I shook my head. I always loathed this city, and this was further proof. I said, "So every time I summon you—"

"Zeyn can zero in on you immediately."

"That could be problematic."

"Perhaps, but you are wily old king. I am certain you can circumvent this using your fox-like cunning."

"Don't patronize me, ifrit. Begone."

"As you wish, master," he said, and although I couldn't see him, I suspected Faddy had bowed deeply, grinning all the way down.

I took Jewel's hand. "We need to go."

"But where?"

"Anywhere but here. And no magic, or djinns."

"So we are forced to live by your wits alone?" she asked, and I heard the mocking in her voice.

"My wits have gotten us this far," I said, scanning the lush gardens. We were in the courtyard of a *caravanserai*, a roadside inn popular with passing caravans, and perhaps not so popular with traveling djinns; at least, not presently. I thought I heard voices coming from the east side of the garden. Indeed, there was a single portal—a pointed arched opening—that led to the streets and wide enough to give access to heavily laden beasts of burden. It was the only entrance into the open courtyard.

"Your wits and my breasts," she snorted.

"We'll talk about your breasts later," I said, and pulled her along. The *caravanserai* was lined with smaller doors that would lead to the building's many rooms.

I led the way across the brick yard, past stalls and niches and bays that would accommodate merchants and pack animals. We stepped around large piles of steaming camel dung and ducked into a doorway just as a troupe of armed guards stormed through the portal. The heavy wooden door was, mercifully, unbarred. I pushed it open and we eased inside just as the guards fanned out.

Inside, the room was absolutely stifling. It also smelled of hay and urine and dirty camel, a nauseating combination not uncommon for these parts.

"They'll be looking for a man and a woman," I said, going through the clothing in the room. Obviously, the renter was away at the moment, perhaps selling his wares in the market stalls that would be located just outside *caravanserai.*

I quickly went through the filthy, dust covered clothing, and selected some of the foulest and handed them to Jewel. She wrinkled her nose and turned her head away.

"They're filthy!"

"We must look the part of road-weary, dust-covered travelers," I said, grinning.

She snatched the clothing from my hand and put them over her own, as I did my own selection. I did not enjoy stealing from those less fortunate, even their filthy clothing, but our lives were more important. The best I could offer was a small prayer, blessing the traveling merchant's wares, and wishing him a robust day of sales.

We both expertly wrapped turbans around our heads, and after tucking away some of Jewel's stray strands, we eased out of the room and into a connecting hallway. Candles flickered and footsteps seemed to echo from everywhere. People were coming. Many people.

Soldiers, I thought grimly.

The hallway would wrap around the entire, perfectly square structure. Following it would be pointless. Eventually, we would run in to soldiers, and I wasn't sure how well our disguises would hold up, filthy or otherwise.

There were, however, adjoining rooms, bigger rooms. Those set apart for the wealthiest of travelers. But these would not be left empty. In the least, these would be manned by servants.

Loud voices were coming from around a far corner, along with the sounds of running boots. What to do? Storm a wealthy merchant's lavish quarters, or face a troop of soldiers?

It was times such as these that I realized how heavily I relied on Faddy. The ifrit could have pointed me to the safest room possible or perhaps find me another means of escape. As it was, I was on my own.

Now came the sounds of doors systematically opening and closing. The soldiers were checking all the rooms. I heard a woman scream, and a soldier grunt. He left her alone and I had an idea.

"Come," I said to Jewel. "Back in the room."

She did as she was told, although she frowned, clearly confused. Once in the room, I clicked shut the heavy door. I immediately began unbuckling the the belt that held up my trousers.

"Now get on your back and lift up your robe."

"You're mad!"

"Perhaps, but we are desperate. You must trust me."

The sound of slamming doors drew closer, followed by the stomping of boots and the demands of soldiers. Jewel looked from the closed door, which would be yanked open at any minute, to a straw bed in the far corner of the room.

In the room next to ours, a door opened, and then slammed shut.

Jewel grimaced and then flung herself to the straw bed. I flung myself on top of her, with my trousers around my ankles. Boots stomped toward our shut door.

I worked my way between her strong but soft legs, pressing my flaccid member against a warmth greater than I had expected. I gasped, and so did Jewel.

And when the door slammed open with such force that it sent shockwaves through the stone floor and straw bed, I was pantomiming the motion of deep lovemaking. We were both mostly dressed in filthy traveling attire, and for all the world—especially to the two guards standing there watching us—we would have looked like a typical husband and wife finding some alone time after days and perhaps weeks of traveling.

Jewel screamed on cue and I grunted like a man lost in the throes of passion. One of the guards grinned and cocked his head and I saw a flash of whitish teeth.

"Carry on, good man," he said, and the two soldiers left, shutting the door far gentler than I would have believed.

"You may get off me now," said Jewel.

And I did, slowly. I hadn't realized how deeply I was holding her in my arms. Surely my pantomime of lovemaking had been a convincing one to the soldiers. As I sat back, with her legs still spread open and her robe pushed up over her flat waist, I saw something shocking.

A mild erection.

Jewel had felt it and gave me a sly grin. "The king returns, after all," she said, standing over me and straightening her robe. She held out her hand. "Now, let's find this cheese merchant friend of yours."

CHAPTER TWENTY

"We'll find the merchant at the bazaar," I said.

"But that's the most public place in the city!" she protested.

I smiled. "Where else would merchants be? We'll have to hurry to reach him before your ex husband's men do."

She nodded. "That should be soon. They'll be asking my son what he wants for his special meal, so they can fetch it by evening. My wretch of a husband, Amir Ibrahim, is very efficient."

We closed dirty hoods about our faces and moved out. There was no sense in either of us risking recognition. The soldiers were still checking out rooms. "Soon they'll realize that we have slipped the noose," I murmured. "We must lose ourselves in the throng."

We did. It was a nice day, and the streets were crowded with shoppers. For once I appreciated the hustle and pushing. Even if the soldiers caught on to our identity, they would have a hard time getting through the throng rapidly to reach us.

It was also oddly private, because no one was paying attention to anyone else; each person was intent on making his own purchases before the choicest items were sold elsewhere. "How do you know we can trust this cheese merchant of yours?" Jewel asked as we pushed along toward the bazaar.

"It's a fair story."

"It's important!" she retorted.

So I told the story. "When I was king I was on a pleasure hunting excursion when we spied a mounted robber band. They knew better than to try to molest us, so behaved politely and we ignored them.

There are so many rogues out there that we don't bother with them unless they become obnoxious."

"And the common man must look out for himself," she said dryly.

I glanced at her. "What's your point?"

She grimaced. "Go on with your story."

"Then we came across a man on the ground. He had evidently been beaten and robbed of his horse. It happened that my son was along, as I was showing him the way of a royal hunt. He jumped off his horse and ran to succor the beaten man. That was his mother's influence, making him feel for anyone's hurts, a nuisance, but once he acted I had to support him so that it would seem that he had acted at my behest. I questioned the man. He turned out to be a merchant returning from the eastern mountain region with rare yak cheese and oriental spices. He had just been waylaid, his goods and horses stolen, and the bandits had abducted his wife and daughter. He begged me to at least save his family.

"'Of course we will,' my son said. Thus I was committed. I sent men after the bandits. We slew the robbers, rescued the woman and daughter, and recovered the horses and merchandise. We returned all of this to him, at my son's insistence. I sent him on his way to town with a special guard so that no other ruffians would molest them. That pleased my son, which was the only reason I did it. We continued with the hunt. But before he left, the merchant swore an oath of gratitude. 'If ever I can repay you in kind, Sire, let me know.' I shrugged it off, but thereafter did business with him, and his gratitude remained."

"You saved his wife and child," Jewel said.

"And later lost my own, ironically. But that is the nature of fate."

She nodded. "I believe he can be trusted to help you. I understand the way he feels."

We were making progress. "The bazaar is up ahead," I said. Then: "When we emulated sex, I began to, to—"

"No mystery there," she said. "It's not incapacity of sex that balks you, but the loss of love. When you recover love, you will recover sex."

"I want to recover it with you. You are more woman than any I have encountered since I lost my wife."

"But as I told you, I am not interested in remarrying. I love only my son."

I saw a potentially useful parallel. "And if your son should come to like me, what then?"

She nodded again. "When your son acted, you had to support him. It would be the same with me."

"And if he wanted you to marry me?"

"You cunning schemer! I could not say no to him. But he's an independent cuss, like his father. I doubt he'll have much use for you." She paused. "But I will restore your virility if you save him. That's all I will promise."

Nevertheless, she had given me the key to her heart. It was her son. The kid might be a brat, but I could court him for the sake of his mother.

Now at last we reached the bazaar. I pointed out the yak cheese merchant, there with his daughter, now a comely girl. "You be a customer while I speak with him privately," I murmured.

"Done."

The booth was bedecked with cheeses and spices. The merchant's girl smiled prettily at Jewel, who smiled back. Meanwhile I nudged close to the merchant. "I have a favor to reclaim," I said.

"Who are you?" he asked sharply.

"Aladdin, incognito," I said, opening my hood to show my face. "Do not react," I added quickly. "I must remain anonymous."

"I hear and obey, my liege," he said recognizing me. "What favor?"

"I am taken with the woman there," I said, flicking my eyes toward Jewel. "Perhaps she will be my new queen. But I must rescue her son from bandits before they sacrifice him to their foul god tonight. For his last meal he will demand yak cheese and chocolate sauce."

"They will come here," the merchant said, catching on. "Only three local merchants carry yak cheese, and the other two are sold out. But chocolate—that is beyond my means. Only the djinni can obtain it."

"The djinni will," I said. "They will bring it here. You must promise to deliver it by evening. You will send your eunuch with it just before the deadline."

"I have no—" He broke off. "Do you mean—?"

"Yes. I will be the eunuch. Do you have a place for me to stay while we wait?"

"I have a shed behind my stall. From there you can overhear what transpires here. It isn't much, but—"

"It will do. Just tell the messengers when they come, and do not give us away. Our lives would be forfeit."

"I understand, Sire. It will be done."

"My gratitude," I said.

"None required, Sire. There is nothing more precious than a child." The merchant signaled his daughter, who broke off and came to him. "These anonymous people will hide in our back shed. Make sure no one knows they are there."

"Yes, father." She turned to me. "If you will come with me, sir."

Jewel and I followed the girl down the crowded street. She led us around the block, then in between buildings, until we came back to the bazaar from behind. No one else could have known where we were going. She indicated a humble shed where unsold goods were stacked. "Here."

We could hear the sounds of the bazaar, but nothing was visible beyond the wall of stalls and goods. There was an aisle to the front, but the merchant had not had us use it lest we be seen.

We entered the shed, and the girl went back the way we had come. "She's a marvel of discretion," Jewel remarked. "I'm glad you saved her."

"She doesn't even remember me."

"Oh, but she does. I saw her eyes glow when she recognized you. She doesn't know why you are here, but she's honored to assist you. She'd jump into bed with you if you wished it."

"She's only ten years old!"

"And your point is?"

I was of course being foolish. Some royals liked children, and the children were thrilled to serve, apart from the rich rewards their families got from such quiet trysts. It paid to please royalty, whatever the manner. But that was not my way.

We lay in the shed. It was hot, but not unbearably. "Now the chocolate," Jewel murmured.

Oh, yes. "But if I rub the lamp here, they'll find us."

"True. So I will remain here and listen, while you get out a fair distance, talk with the lamp, and return."

That made sense. I left her in the shed and made my way out to the far street, which fortunately was not crowded. I walked swiftly to another street where there were horses and wagons waiting. Then I rubbed the lamp. "Do not show yourself," I said as I did.

"I am here," Lamprey said.

"Fetch a small jug of chocolate sauce and take it to the merchant's stall we just visited. Do not give any evidence of your nature, so that those who are tracking the invocation of the lamp are not alerted. Can you do that?" I figured a jug was not a complicated transport, so his powers would not be strained. Supernatural creatures abounded, so the soldiers would not be going after incidental ones, merely the ones I summoned.

"On my way," the djinn said.

I returned to the shed, lingering just long enough to see the soldiers racing toward the spot where I had used the lamp. That gave me an idea how long it took to zero in on my magic. They were uncomfortably prompt.

I faded out of sight. I heard the horses neighing as soldiers charged among them. Soon there would be chaos as the soldiers searched for what was not there, and realized that their quarry had slipped the noose again and might even be deliberately teasing them. They might take it out on the horses, which would incite a near riot as furious wagoners retaliated. Still, it would be best if the chocolate were delivered promptly so we could get out of here.

"It has been delivered," Jewel said.

"Already?" But of course time was as nothing to the djinn.

"Then my plan to rescue your son is on track," I said, relieved.

We lay together, waiting for the next stage. "About your manhood," Jewel said. "It may take time to restore it completely, but let's see if we can advance it a stage."

"I don't know. That emulation we did may have been a fluke."

"I think not. You are healing, my lord." She reached into my trousers. Then, holding on, she kissed me. I felt a stirring such as I had not had in a long time. She knew what she was doing.

Now there were voices from the stall. "Yak cheese I have, honored sir. But chocolate? That would take me a week to obtain."

"You will have it by midnight tonight, or your head will be ground up to take its place."

"But sir! It's impossible!"

"You will make it possible."

"And how am I to pay my supplier for it? Genuine chocolate is fabulously expensive."

"Will this help?" It had to be a huge amount of gold.

"I will have my eunuch deliver it tonight," the merchant promised.

"Some other time," Jewel said with seeming regret, putting my member away. "We have my son to rescue."

Indeed we did. I almost wished it had taken the enemy longer to come to the merchant. Because I knew that rescuing the boy was unlikely to be as straightforward as I had presented it.

CHAPTER TWENTY-ONE

As pleasurable as it was lying with Jewel in that hidden shed, there was little time to waste. After all, I had yak milk and chocolate to deliver. And a son to save.

The guards had further instructed the merchant to have his eunuch deliver the goods to the Temple of the Moon, a stone structure found at the bottom of a deep valley and carved directly into a cliff face. It was a structure that was known to me, and not one I was pleased to hear included. After all, Death is said to abide in that temple, one of his many earthly homes. The valley itself is found just outside of the city, perhaps less than a day's ride by horse. Plenty of time to deliver the goods by midnight.

With the sun beginning its descent into the western sky, Jewel and I sat in the shade of an outdoor cafe with Sa'ood. Across the way, his daughter tended to their stall—and even from here I could hear the child expertly haggle with their many customers, all of whom were far older than she. The young girl drove a hard bargain. Obviously, she been taught by the best, Sa'ood himself.

"I am very proud of her," said the merchant, sipping his hot tea and watching his daughter. "And she would not be here, if not for you, my liege."

The truth was, of course, it had been my son's bleeding heart who had led me to save Sa'ood and his family. Admittedly, I had been selfish in my youth, especially when I had found the lamp; indeed, it is easy to be self-serving when the world is at your fingertips. But witnessing my son's compassion on a nearly daily basis had made me a better man.

Sa'ood turned his attention back to me. "You are aware that this temple is the legendary home of Death."

I nodded, drinking my own bitter coffee. I kept a look-out for more soldiers, but it had been some time since I last rubbed the lamp. "One of his many homes," I said. "Perhaps he is summering elsewhere."

Sa'ood frowned at my flippancy. "There is another legend concerning the stone temple."

"How many legends are there?" snorted Jewel.

"Samarkand is full of legends, my dear, some more pervasive than others. This next one is more of a prophecy, but it is one that is well known among Samarkanders."

I nodded, suspecting what he had to say. "Not just in Samarkand," I said. "But beyond. A great magician would emerge from the Temple of the Moon on the night of two moons."

"A night of two moons?" said Jewel, frowning. "I do not understand."

But I thought I understood, and did my best to explain. The Islamic calendar consisted of twelve full lunar cycles. In addition to those twelve cycles, each solar calendar year contained roughly eleven days more than the lunar year of twelve lunations. The extra days accumulate, and when they add up to roughly thirty days, which is about every three years, the Islamic calendar accounts for those days with "leap months". It is in such months that an extra full moon occurs, once every three years.

"And we are in such a month," I said. "With an extra full moon."

"A month with two full moons," said Jewel.

I nodded. "And tonight is the second full moon."

"A night of two moons."

I nodded again. "It appears tonight is of significance, perhaps in more ways than one."

"So who is this magician?" asked Jewel.

"My guess would be Zeyn," I said. "He's certainly the greatest magician, or sorcerer, in Djinnland."

"So we have even more reason to stop him," said Jewel, "although saving my son would certainly be enough for me."

The sun had dipped a little more, angling straight into our faces. The city of Samarkand appeared deceptively serene. Dark magic abounded, and a curse lay over the land, of that I was sure.

"So what is the plan?" asked Jewel.

"I will arrive on horseback with the requested items."

"And where will I be?" asked Jewel.

"You will be here, with Sa'ood and his daughter, selling cheese. Perhaps you can pick up a new trade."

Sa'ood chuckled, but Jewel threw me a furious look. "If you think for one minute that I will wait here and do nothing—"

"Oh, but you won't be doing nothing," I said easily. "You will be helping my good man sell his fine cheeses."

"Aladdin—"

"Not so loud, my dear. I'm incognito, remember?"

"But perhaps I can travel with you, in Lamprey's lamp, and once we arrive, you can summon me—"

I shook my head. "Even to get you in the lamp we would alert the guards, and to summon you again would alert them further."

"Then what will you do once you arrive? You are but one man. Surely my ex-husband will have many soldiers with him, in addition to Zeyn's magic."

I sipped my bitter coffee and sat back, one arm draped over the back of the wooden chair. "Oh, I am certain I will think of something, my dear."

She bit her tongue. For once, Jewel was without opinion or leverage. We finished our drinks in silence and then we loaded up my pack horse. With Sa'ood's guidance, I had a firm understanding of the necessary route I would take to the valley temple, and as I stepped up into the saddle and swung my leg around, Jewel came to my side. There were tears in her eyes.

"Be careful, my lord," she said.

"Oh, I plan on being careful, especially since I plan to return with your son and marry you."

She gave me a sad smile. "I care only about my son and his safety, my lord."

"I, too, care only about your son and his safety, my *queen*," I said, and I lifted her face toward me gently and we kissed for a long, long time.

CHAPTER TWENTY-TWO

Sa'ood's daughter finished with her sale and turned to him. "This plan won't work, father."

Because the girl's doubts echoed mine, I reluctantly separated myself from Jewel. What did the girl know?

"This is not your concern, Myrrh," he snapped. I was interested to note that he had evidently named her after one of the precious condiments he carried along with his exotic cheeses and spices. Myrrh had a bitter scent, but was used in perfume, and was quite rare and valuable. It was surely a fitting name.

"Oh, but it is, father. They are lurking to capture, bind, and torture our liege, to make him do their bidding. He must not ride into their trap."

Sa'ood focused on her. "I did not tell you his identity."

"I knew it before he came to us, father."

Sa'ood turned to me. "I must apologize for my daughter. She has second sight, sometimes."

"Second sight?" I asked.

"She can see into the future. When she and my wife were abducted, she told her mother not to worry, because we would be rescued soon, at the behest of the king's son. But it's not reliable."

"But that's exactly what happened," I said.

"Yes. But she also said she was going to marry the king's son, who would be a great magician. Then—" He shrugged, not wanting to refer directly to the fate of my wife and son.

How well I understood. My son was dead.

"They tried to use the king's son to gain power over the king," Myrrh said. "But they botched it, and killed him and his mother instead."

"That was part of the conspiracy?" I asked, appalled.

"Now they are trying again, more carefully," Myrrh said. "You must not let them prevail, my liege."

"So you see, sire, sometimes she is right, sometimes she is wrong," Sa'ood said. "She's probably guessing."

"I am not wrong," Myrrh said firmly. "It's just that when it's the far future, the details can be cloudy. I will still marry the king's magician son, when we come of age. He must be rescued now."

"It is *my* son we are rescuing," Jewel said. "He is not the king's son."

"Not yet," the girl replied succinctly.

Jewel and I exchanged a glance. If we rescued the boy, and Jewel married me, and I became king again, I would of course adopt the boy. He would become the king's son.

"My son," Jewel said, a new realization dawning. "I thought they meant to sacrifice him while he remained an innocent child, before his manhood came upon him."

"That, too," Myrrh said. "But mainly they do not want him to achieve his magician power, to rival theirs."

Shaken, I turned to Sa'ood. "I think your daughter's power is valid. We need her help."

"We do," Jewel agreed.

"But she's a child!" the merchant protested. "She doesn't know about the ugliness of adult politics."

"Father, without the king's intercession, I would today be a young temple whore, and mother an old one. Now without my intercession, the king's second son and my future husband will die tonight."

"So much for childish innocence," Jewel murmured.

I faced Myrrh. "I have two djinn I can summon, but neither is at present strong enough to help significantly, and the act of summoning them will betray our presence to the enemy. So I must not use magic until the last possible moment. What do you recommend?"

"I must go with you, my liege, to clarify my vision of immediate events. I can take you there via a secret route that few know of, so that they do not see you coming."

"But I must bring them the cheese and chocolate," I said. "They are expecting the merchant's eunuch to deliver them."

"They know your ruse," the girl said. "The real ruse is theirs, to bring you to them, since their other traps have failed."

"But if I don't bring the cheese and chocolate, I won't get a chance to rescue the boy."

Myrrh glanced impatiently at Jewel, as if to say "This idiot is my future father in law?" Then she faced me. "Let someone else deliver the goods, while you strike unexpectedly to free the boy."

It occurred to me that this savvy girl would make a good daughter-in-law. "Who else would risk dealing with these dangerous men?"

"I will do it," Sa'ood said. "It is my delivery to arrange."

"But you have a business to run," I said.

"Only because you saved my goods and my family from loss, my liege. This is simple enough to do."

I glanced at Myrrh, but she did not protest. The man still felt he owed me.

Neither did Jewel. "I am coming with you too," she said firmly. "My son knows me better than he knows you."

What could I say? That I preferred to travel alone with an obliging girl child? I dismounted, returning the horse to Sa'ood.

Thus it fell into place. With strategy and sufficient fortune we would surprise Zeyn's party and achieve our mission.

Sa'ood took the merchandise and mounted the horse. He set off down the street, making no secret of his presence. Meanwhile we rented horses of our own.

Myrrh led Jewel and me on a devious route through alleys and back streets, and then along a deserted trail into an abandoned wilderness region. I wore a scimitar the merchant had rummaged from his stores, relieved to be armed again. There was no telling what might lurk in a wasteland like this.

"That is a brave thing your father is doing, serving as decoy," Jewel said to Myrrh.

"He is a brave man," the girl agreed. "Fortunately he is not in danger. They will accept his explanation that his eunuch ran away in fear. They know the king will make an appearance before the boy is sacrificed."

"They will have the boy hidden and under guard," I said. "Can you locate him?"

"Yes."

"Here is my plan," I said. "I must reach the boy, persuade him that I represent his mother—"

"No problem there," Jewel said. "I will be with you when you find him."

"Then have us all be conjured into the lamp, so that Lamprey can conjure us to safety. The magic will alert them to our presence, but it will be too late to stop the rescue. Do you think that will work?" Because now I valued her precognition.

"Yes."

There had to be a catch. "Are there any complications we need to be aware of?"

"Just one," Myrrh said. "He is in a locked chamber, in the temple carved from stone, deep in the mountain, under armed guard. I know where he is, but I don't know how to get safely into it. There is no back access to the temple itself."

"I will figure out a way," I said with false confidence.

Jewel gave me a glance that said "You had better."

"This way," Myrrh said. "Quickly."

"But we have a clear trail ahead," I protested.

"Don't argue with her," Jewel said. "She knows what she's doing."

So we deviated from the easy path and made our way up a tortuous detour that ended in a blank face on the slope of the mountain. "This is impassible," I said, disgusted. Our mounts were clearly exhausted.

Jewel nudged me. I followed her look.

Down the ragged slope was the trail we had been following. A small creature was walking along it, going in the opposite direction to ours.

"That's just a stray dog," I said.

"Watch it closely," Myrrh said.

Then I saw the patch of white foam on its muzzle. "Who happens to be rabid," I concluded.

"No safe way to fight or stop that," Jewel said. "We simply had to be where it isn't."

Now I understood. It was a persuasive demonstration of Myrrh's ability. She had seen the cur coming, as it were, and taken evasive action.

We gave the dog time to clear, then made our way cautiously back down the path to the main trail. Our horses uneasily sniffed the trail; they knew what had passed there. Fortunately the animal had never been aware of us, so had not followed us up the slope. Probably its sense of smell was damaged by its malady, so it had missed us. Someone else would suffer that encounter.

We resumed our travel. I glanced nervously back, but Myrrh assured me that the animal was not coming back.

"That cur reminds me of my ex-husband," Jewel murmured.

I had to laugh, knowing she meant in nature rather than appearance. Still, it was another suggestion of the kind of enemy we faced: madness might be easier to deal with. And what about this prophecy of a great magician emerging? I could handle a man with a scimitar, but magic was different. The thing about prophecies was that they always came true, though not necessarily in quite the way expected.

Then suddenly the barren landscape gave way to an awesome cliff overlooking the hidden valley. There across the way was the dread Temple of the Moon.

How could we ever get into that, unobserved? There was only the guarded front entrance, and maybe a servant's access to the side. A narrow trail led down the face of the cliff to the valley floor, so we could get there, but then what?

CHAPTER TWENTY-THREE

We considered our options, and it was Jewel who had the most convincing argument. "The sun is setting and they're going to sacrifice my boy tonight. There's not a thing we can do up here."

And she set off, on her own, down the winding trail. She was a mother who would not be denied. I knew then that part of my challenge was not so much to save her son but to keep Jewel alive as well. She was clearly reckless and desperate, and I didn't fault her for that at all.

I looked at Myrrh and the girl gave me a half smile. I did not need second sight to know that what was about to happen in our immediate future would be a delicate balance of luck and fate. Like with Faddy and Lamprey, one can come to rely too much on such talents. Sometimes, as Jewel had recklessly shown, it is time to act.

Myrrh and I angled our own mounts down the treacherously narrow trail. I have never had a fear of heights; indeed, flying high above the land on nothing more than a rug had been exhilarating. But my mount's maddening tendency to walk on the far edge of the rocky path was having a strange effect on my testicles. With each loose pebble that spilled over the ledge, falling hundreds of feet straight down, and with each dubious step that seemed closer and closer to the edge, my testicles seemed to rise into my stomach to hide like frightened mice.

It would not be very heroic to shut my eyes and so I forced myself to stare at Jewel, who was still twenty or thirty lengths ahead of us. She had yet to look back, assuming we would follow. Little did she know that I would follow her to the ends of the earth.

To distract myself, I looked back at Myrrh. If the young girl had a fear of heights, she didn't show it; indeed, if anything, she seemed lost in thought. No doubt lost in her own second sight. I was tempted to ask what she saw as our chances for survival, but declined. Some things were best unknown, and I knew the power of suggestion.

Instead, I said, "Your father mentioned that, in the past, your second sight was not very reliable. And yet, as far as I can tell, you have proven to be spot on. What has changed?"

She nudged her dust-covered horse a little closer to me. My horse moved to one side to make room, unfortunately, even closer to the far edge. I inadvertently gasped as the frightened mice sought refuge even higher up into my stomach.

Myrrh grinned. "Do not worry, my liege. You will not fall."

The girl's perceptive abilities were off the charts. I wondered if, also, she was telepathic or a mind reader. Often one with such abilities had many other abilities, too. Some of which they rarely admitted to.

The girl suddenly gave me a wry smile, and I suspected I was close in my assumption. She shrugged as if I had asked her a question, and I knew she was being coy.

You can hear my thoughts, young lady, can't you? I thought.

Perhaps, came a small voice in the back of my mind that could have been my own, but I suspected otherwise.

You are a girl of many talents, I thought.

But this is not a talent I readily admit to, came a long string of words, and I knew now that the girl was speaking directly into my mind.

I can see why, I said. *It is is better to have those around you not guard their thoughts.*

A voice giggled in my head, and then said, *As if they could. But, yes, mind reading has helped keep us alive, and has helped us sell a lot of cheese.*

I laughed at this. Yes, indeed, knowing your customer's set price beforehand would be invaluable.

Your secret is safe with me, I thought.

Good. This can be an invaluable service to you, as well, my lord.

Of that I had no doubt. I thought: *But you have not answered my question.*

It is true, came the sweetly innocent words. *My talents and abilities have been spotty in the past, but they seem to be becoming more reliable. But it is like anything. On some days your swordplay might be razor sharp. On other days, you might be listless and dull. It also depends on the circumstances. In this particular case, saving Jewel's son is of great importance to me, and so the second sight comes to me clearly and powerfully, although much remains to be seen, in more ways than one.*

I thought about that, and I knew she could probably read my thoughts, but I also suspected that such mind reading was of great effort to her.

Right again, my liege. I have my own thoughts to think. There isn't time enough in the day to constantly be aware of more than my own. And besides, I feel a particular affinity for you. You saved my family, and now you will save my future husband.

Aw, I thought, *so we will be successful.*

There are three likely outcomes that I can foresee, she thought. *All have equal probability. Success will ultimately be determined, I believe, on your love for Jewel, your cunning, and your resourcefulness.*

And perhaps you? I suggested.

Oh, I couldn't hurt, she giggled.

We broke off our mental dialogue, and shortly, as the sun was now nearly hidden behind the western foothills, we mercifully reached the bottom. My frightened mice dropped back into their proper place.

Jewel was waiting impatiently for us in the shadows of an overhang. With her jaw set and her lips a thin line, she looked as fierce and determined as ever. I knew it was taking all of her control to wait and not to charge forward.

She was a desperate mother, but she was not foolish. From around the overhang, I saw that the narrow path opened into a wide valley floor that led directly to the Temple of the Moon. Guards were there. Many of them, in fact. Their armor and weapons gleamed in the last of the sunlight.

And high above, as if on cue, the full moon seemed to suddenly appear in the southern sky. What now?

"There's only one way in for official visitors," said Jewel. "And it's heavily guarded."

I glanced at Myrrh and I suspected she had read my thoughts, or, in the very least, surmised what I was about to ask. "I do not believe there is another entrance we can use."

Good enough for me, but how would we get in?

Now I was certain she was reading my thoughts. Three words appeared in my mind: *Wait for it.*

I waited, and Jewel did so impatiently. I set a hand on her forearm and she flinched. "We will save him," I said. "But we need patience."

"For what?" she snapped.

And then we saw it or, rather, heard it. Coming from the valley floor to our right, heading toward the Temple of the Moon, was a group of riders on horseback. I didn't need second sight to know who they were. Officials of some sort, here to participate in the ceremony. My anger bubbled over. They were here, of course, to witness the sacrifice of the boy. Who were these people, I did not know, obviously friends of Jewel's ex-husband, those who hoped to share in his dark power and his supposed rise to the throne.

The party was coming around a bend, and not yet visible to the soldiers, but quite visible to us. The narrow path we had followed down was, in effect, the perfect ambush point. I secretly wondered if Myrrh had known this. I glanced at her but she was looking ahead, her eyes glazed, and I suspected her thoughts were elsewhere presently.

The ambush idea had me thinking. I was about to turn to Jewel when Myrrh's hand snaked out and grabbed my arm. "Good idea; bad timing."

"What are you talking about?" snapped Jewel, unaware that Myrrh and I had just communicated telepathically.

"I was just thinking out loud, Amira," she said, addressing Jewel with her formal title. After all, if everything worked out, Jewel could very well be the girl's mother-in-law.

Another thought for another time. I wasn't sure whose words those were. Myrrh's or mine.

"I sensed my lord's desire to ambush this party and to take their place, but I sense great strength and much dark magic within this group. It would be better to wait."

Jewel nodded suspiciously. The woman was, perhaps, more perceptive than I had given her credit for. Clearly she did not fully accept Myrrh's explanation. When all this was said and done, I would see about convincing Myrrh to include Jewel into our small circle of telepathy.

Perhaps, came the single word.

And so we waited. The first group pushed on, while we hid in the shadows. A second group appeared. A smaller party. Indeed, there were only three of them.

This was our chance.

CHAPTER TWENTY-FOUR

I drew my scimitar. "Stay back," I told Jewel and Myrrh grimly. "This may get messy."

"Don't," Jewel said. "A fracas will attract attention from the guards at the temple, the last thing we want."

"Those travelers are not going to yield their places voluntarily," I pointed out. "This is an important event."

"And how will we emulate them if we don't know who they are?" Jewel asked. "The temple surely has a list."

She had a point, unfortunately. "You have a better way?"

"I do," Myrrh said. "I have powdered bhang my father uses for difficult negotiations. One sniff will put a man into a pleasant daze for a few minutes, during which time he will answer questions and be amenable to suggestions. We can learn what we need and be off before they realize."

"And when they do realize, what then?" I asked dubiously. I knew of bhang, of course; it derived from hemp and had pacifying and hallucinogenic properties. It had been a palace staple when I was king, useful for making resistive maidens amenable, the beauty of it being that they seldom actually remembered what had transpired during the session. There had been the lovely chaste daughter of a visiting king from the infidel kingdom of France, fair game of course since they were not true believers, but they did have a barbarian hangup about virginity. News of my lust for her would have meant war. What a delight she had been for a night, thanks to bhang! If she remembered, she never told, and there was no war. Not something I'm proud of, and certainly not my finest hour. I had let my power and lust cloud my better judgment. My wife had not approved, obviously; true, rulers often did have a harem, and I was no different, but it had been politically dangerous, she said. She thought I should have confined my incidental passions to girls of the faith. She did have a point; infidels were socially unclean.

"By then we will be inside the temple," Myrrh said. "The real party will be barred as impostors, since the listed envoy will already have been admitted."

"But surely the temple authorities will be suspicious," Jewel said.

"And admit they made a mistake?" I retorted. "Not likely. Guards who make mistakes may be required to publicly eat their own intestines."

"Also, my father will arrive just after we do," Myrrh said. "That will be a distraction."

Jewel's lips quirked. "I could get to like you, girl. You have a sensible mind."

"That's good," Myrrh said. "We will have a long and close association, once the uncertainties of this night are resolved."

"You don't know that they will be resolved in our favor?"

"When there is the involvement of a powerful magician, I can't be sure of anything. Reality changes in the vicinity of such men. But we have a fair chance."

Meanwhile the party was getting close. "Get your powder ready," I told Myrrh.

"Hail, stranger!" the leading figure called.

"Hail," I agreed. "We must talk." We rode toward them.

"It is a great event we anticipate," the other said. "I am the vizier of Shams al-Din Muhammad from Egypt, come to swear fealty to the new magician-king on behalf of my lord."

"Early subscribers will be richly rewarded," I agreed, suppressing a surge of rage. The impostor was already accepting the fealty of my long-time allies?

Then Myrrh held up a little squeeze bag. "Hold your breath until it dissipates," she murmured. Then she squeezed. A faint haze puffed out, wafting toward the other party. The girl had evidently made note of the breeze.

I unobtrusively held my breath, as did Jewel and Myrrh.

"They will indeed," Shams said jovially. He took a breath. "I didn't hear your name." His hand rested not far from his scimitar.

Then his eyes became vague. So did those of his two companions.

I waited until the haze had passed on behind them. "Who are your companions?" I asked.

"My porter and body servant." I saw that the porter's horse was loaded with practical travel things like blankets and pots, and the servant's steed carried items of tonsure and hygiene. They had probably traveled with a larger caravan most of the way, then peeled off for this private mission.

"Stay here," I told him. That should keep this party here until the bhang wore off. Then to Jewel: "I will be the vizier from Egypt. You will be my porter, and Myrrh my body servant. Can you emulate a man?"

She brought out a handful of rouge and rubbed it across her chin so that she looked light-bearded. She tied back her hair so that it did not show. She assumed a sour look. That would do.

"Give me your vizier's badge," I told the man from Egypt. That would be our entry pass.

He handed it over without protest. Bhang was wonderful stuff.

We rode on toward the palace. The larger preceding party had just been processed in, and the guards were ready for us. Now I saw that they had a brace of trained dogs. That could be mischief.

One guard stepped forward to intercept us as we dismounted and turned our horses over to the waiting stablehands. "State your name, office, and identity of your companions."

"I am the vizier of Shams al-Din Muhammad from Egypt, come to swear fealty to the new magician-king on behalf of my lord," I said, repeating the line by rote. I could do that when I needed to; it came with having diplomatic experience. "These are my porter and body servant." I held out my badge of authority.

The two dogs sniffed our robes. One made a little half whining sound.

Now the guard sniffed too. "Perfume!" he said. "There's a woman nigh."

And women were normally mere auxiliaries, not persons of power. Mischief indeed. "And what if there is?" I demanded.

"No woman enters by this gate," the guard said. "Such lowly chattel enter only by the side door, for scullery, maid, or whore duties."

That was the entry we had not been able to use, because any visitor approaching the servant's door would attract unwelcome suspicion.

Jewel was swelling up, being no maid or whore. I had to defuse this in a hurry. "So my porters are women," I said. "Also my cook and body servant. I trust no other with my personal business. They stay with me."

But in my feigned indignation I had let my hood fall open. The guard stared at my face. "King Aladdin!"

Oh, camel crap! I would never be able to explain this away. They were of course alert for my arrival.

NO!

I recognized the mental voice. It was Myrrh.

The guard stood as if bemused. Then he blinked. His features clarified. "State your name, office, and identity of your companions."

It was the opening challenge. I realized that Myrrh had discovered and invoked another magic ability: blotting out a thought. She had erased the guard's recognition of me, and perhaps also the awareness of the gender of my two companions. We could do this over, correctly.

But we were running out of time, because now the party we had replaced was approaching. We had to get clear before they caught up and gave us the lie.

And another rider was coming from the other direction. That was Sa'ood, bringing the cheese and chocolate. I saw that the guard knew his mission and wanted to get clear of us. If we could just oblige him in time.

PASS, VIZIER OF EGYPT. That was Myrrh again, projecting a thought.

"Pass, vizier of Egypt," the guard said formally, not questioning what he took to be his own thought.

We stepped forward, passing through the dread portal of the Temple of the Moon as the guards addressed the other arrivals.

Now it was time for the hard part of our mission. Before they caught on to our presence, and the dung hit the wall.

CHAPTER TWENTY-FIVE

We joined a long receiving line that wound slowly through a stunning stone temple carved from the face of the cliff.

I had little time to admire the marvelous feat of human engineering. Instead, I was alert for an opportunity to slip away. Behind us, I heard a small commotion, and I knew the real vizier of Egypt had arrived. It would only be a matter of moments before they would come looking for us; in the very least, to straighten out the confusion.

That guard had readily recognized me. He wouldn't be the only one. Many here would have known me back in the day, which was why I kept my head down, permitting the headcloth I was wearing to partially obscure my features. Mercifully, the temple was mostly dark, lit only with flickering torches along the walls. Sounds echoed from seemingly everywhere, the result of the acoustics of the massive room. Amazingly, there seemed to be rooms within rooms. Perhaps the temple had been originally carved from a natural cavern and tunnel network, which made more sense, and would take less time.

The line, I saw, plunged through a pointed archway and into a brightly lit chamber. Firelight danced within. Smoke drifted through the room, stinging the eyes. People were scattered about here and there, talking amiably. Perhaps these folk had already greeted whoever was waiting at the end of the line. And I was beginning to suspect I knew who was waiting at the end of the line: Jewel's ex-husband.

You would be correct, sire, came the words in my mind.

Have you been listening the whole time? I asked.

Your thoughts and mine, in this situation and at this time, are unusually connected. Perhaps because we are going to need each other if we are to survive this.

Fine, I thought. *Do you sense where the boy is?*

He is beyond, deeper in the tunnel system. My liege, I sense great magic here. More than I have ever felt before. There is something powerful in this temple.

Zeyn was here, of course. Hidden perhaps. Or with the boy.

I turned to Jewel, who was looking increasingly agitated. I didn't blame her. The voices were growing louder behind us, as the real vizier had clearly lost his composure. Probably not a good idea to lose one's cool in a secret blood ceremony of heads of state. Someone was going to get their own head chopped off, and it wasn't going to be mine.

"Let's go," I said, and took Jewel's arm.

We casually stepped out of line and worked our way over to where other officials were chatting quietly under a flickering torch. Although this was a ceremony of the darkest magic, which included a human sacrifice, it was also deeply political. No head of state would be here in any official capacity. Indeed, a ceremony like this would only attract those who wished to undermine the current rulers, those who wished to align themselves with a dark power, hoping to gain such power themselves. Perhaps there were some here who had no clue what was going on. Perhaps these would be sacrificed as well. I did not know, and could not, but I doubted that all was as it seemed.

You are closer than you think, my liege, came the words. *Although I am young and do not fully understand the politics of man, I do know there are some here who are unaware of the full implications tonight will bring.*

And what are those implications? I thought.

Tonight, a ruler will be named and a great magician revealed.

Unless we stop them, I thought.

But she said nothing, frowning. Perhaps even she was uncertain of her own prognostications. Finally her words appeared in my mind: *We will see, my liege.*

"Pretend we're chatting casually," I whispered, adopting a formal and relaxed demeanor.

"Of course, my liege," said Jewel, trailing me slightly, as did Myrrh. To any and all concerned, we appeared as any other small group as we awaited the grand ceremony that would be starting soon. She added, "And what do you propose we do?"

"We need to find another way out of here."

From behind us, the vizier raised his voice, demanding something or other. This was followed by a long, gurgling scream, and the vizier demanded no more.

Now guards pushed past us, running toward the entrance. It would be only a matter of minutes before they came looking for us. Even routine questioning would be catastrophic for our quest. No doubt I would be recognized instantly, and I was certain Myrrh's mind-trick wouldn't work on very many people at once.

You are correct, sire.

Someday, you are going to have to get out of my mind.

Someday, sire.

The guards, I saw, had abandoned their post in front of a narrow doorway. To where it led, I had no clue, but it was the only alternative we had to the reception line entering the main chamber, where, I assumed, the sacrifice would take place.

Quickly, I steered Jewel and Myrrh through the doorway and, with a discreet look around to verify we had gone unnoticed, into a very dark passageway. And since the girl had not protested, I assumed I had chosen the correct path. Either way, I trusted my instincts in such matters. Perhaps well-honed instincts were just as good as a powerful sixth sense.

Or perhaps, came her innocent words, *they are one and the same.*

At the far end of the dark tunnel there was a bright light. Behind us, through the tunnel opening, I heard muffled voices. Had we been seen entering through the doorway after all? I didn't know, but I wasn't going to wait to find out.

We hurried down the tunnel, moving blindly in the dark. Mercifully the passageway was smooth underfoot, with no irregularities or random overhangs to knock us unconscious. I also noted the absence of cobwebs. The tunnel had been used recently. For what purpose, I did not know.

And what was waiting for us at the far end, I did not know either. But we were about to find out.

CHAPTER TWENTY-SIX

I paused, my natural caution coming into play. "Myrrh, can you fathom what's ahead?"

The girl concentrated. "Just a matron, in charge of domestic arrangements for the boy. Food, bedding, waste disposal, and she alerts the authorities if anything unusual occurs. She's really frustrated."

"So my son is close," Jewel said eagerly.

"Yes. But there are other guards at his chamber. We can't just take out the matron and go to him."

I zeroed in on something potentially useful. "Why is she frustrated? No virile man in her life?"

Myrrh exchanged a glance with Jewel. I needed no mind reading to understand it: why did men always think of sex? They never thought to ask the obvious corollary: why *didn't* women? Then Myrrh answered. "No, sire. She's frustrated that the fine hot meal she prepared is getting cold, because the cheese and chocolate are late arriving. She can't even reheat it until she knows the cheese is there. She's steaming; she could just about heat the food without fire."

Jewel glanced at me. "She has reason. So what's the plan, genius?"

It burst upon me. "You and I need to hide until we can reach your son unobserved. We need simple menial tasks to mask our real identities, since they are searching for us. That search is what's messing up the delivery of the meal. So I will be the garbage disposal lout, you will be the food deliverer, and Myrrh the messenger girl." I looked at Myrrh. "You can make the matron accept that as reasonable?"

"Yes. But I'd better be the deliverer. If Jewel tries to take the food in, those guards—well, they're men. To them, serving wenches are for them to play with while they wait on the boy eating his meal."

"I can handle men," Jewel said grimly.

"But you won't have any good place to dispose of the bodies, and when they don't make their regular reports, the authorities will know and converge."

Jewel nodded. "Point made. I'll help heat the food. You deliver, and tell my son that his rescue is nigh."

"I will try."

"You can whisper so the guards don't hear."

"It's not that. It's that I have touched his mind. He has been—his mind has been clouded so he doesn't know he's a prisoner. If I try to tell him, he may alert the guards. Then *I'll* become their diversion."

That made Jewel pause. "Yes, of course they would lie to him. But can you communicate mentally, to tell him what really happened?"

"I can try, if I can make him pay attention to me."

"Oh come on, Myrrh! You're a *woman.*"

Now Myrrh nodded. "Or I will be soon. And he will soon be a man. Maybe I can put the thought of our future love in his mind, so he focuses properly on me."

"Do it. If there's one thing that can cut through a man's clouds, it's the suggestion of the favor of a woman. Put the hook in; lead him by the nose." Her mouth quirked. "Or whatever."

"As you have been leading Aladdin," Myrrh agreed. "Now I see the way."

I had to agree. I had picked up on Jewel's sexual ambiance the moment I first saw her, and she had kept my close attention ever since. "Then we have our plan," I said. "Except for one thing: how will we know when to strike, as we won't be with Myrrh when she persuades your son?"

"I will connect your minds to mine," Myrrh said. "I believe I can do that now, because I am coming to know you well. So you will both see and hear what I am perceiving, and will know when the time is right."

Then she demonstrated by showing us ourselves through her eyes, standing there in the tunnel. I looked like a disreputable tramp and Jewel's face was still smudged to make her look masculine. Myrrh could indeed do it.

Jewel and I both nodded. Our plan was complete.

Reminded of her appearance, Jewel found a cloth and wiped her face, becoming feminine again. "I'd rather be a woman anyway," she murmured. "But you look perfect as a lout."

"Thank you," I said ironically.

We marched on into the light.

The matron looked up. "At last! The chocolate!"

"Not yet," Jewel said. "Strangers crashed the gate, and the guards are searching for them, disrupting everything, and the schedule got messed up. But it's on the way. We're the service crew."

"Well go back and get it!" the matron snapped.

"Go get it, girl," Jewel told Myrrh.

"And you, wench, get the hearth fire blazing," the matron said to Jewel. She turned to me. "And you haul off the refuse, lout." The woman was evidently accustomed to handling desultory servants.

Myrrh obediently went back down the passage. I oriented on the refuse can, identifying it by the smell. Rotting food, urine, turds, and whatever else that was spoiling: a potent combination. No one would inspect me too closely, because of the stench. I picked it up and started carrying it toward the tunnel.

"Not that way, idiot!" the matron snapped. "Use the back passage to the service entrance." She gestured to another tunnel.

I reversed course and entered the new tunnel. It was gloomy, but burning torches were spaced along it so I could see. This was exactly what I wanted: to explore the back passages we might need for escape, in case anything went wrong. Or, rather, *when* everything went wrong.

The images from Myrrh's eyes had faded when she focused on the matron, to make sure the woman saw nothing wrong with our presence. Now they resumed, and though I still had my own vision, as I trudged slowly along the passage with my stinking load, I also saw a view of another passage. Myrrh was coming to the light of the main hall.

People were still running around in a kind of organized chaos, but now a guard was bringing in the cheese and chocolate. I could tell because Myrrh peeked at the mind of the guard to verify it. "I'll take that," she said briskly as he came up.

"But I am to deliver it only to—"

"Me," she said, taking it. The guard looked perplexed, and faintly dazed, and I knew she had sent him a thought. That was marvelous power she had!

Myrrh carried the package back through the tunnel to the matron. "Let's see it," the matron said, having evidently learned never to take anything for granted. She checked, and saw that it was good yak cheese, with a vial of brown syrup. She broke off a fragment of cheese and tasted it, verifying its quality, and shook a drop of sauce onto her palm, touching her tongue to it. She was thorough, the kind of servant a king could trust. "It will do."

Jewel had the fire going, and the main part of the meal was hot. The matron, responsive to a command she did not know she was receiving, prepared a platter with the several items upon it, and gave it to Myrrh. "Take it in to the brat, and see that he eats it." She winked. "There's a bit of bhang in the soup; he won't be any trouble for the night's event."

Jewel and Myrrh must have kept straight faces, because the matron evinced no alarm. She had no notion how she was flirting with death in this temple of death. Jewel would gladly have gutted her, had she been able to do so with impunity. But I knew the woman was acting under orders. Just as bhang made a difficult maiden amenable in bed, it made a victim amenable to sacrifice, to a degree, depending on the dose. It was a prudent measure.

Myrrh walked on into the passage leading to the boy's prison, carrying the covered platter. I continued hauling my garbage. I no longer saw Jewel, because Myrrh was no longer with her, but I knew she was busy being an obedient servant. She was doing what was necessary, biding her time until Myrrh gave the call. I knew she was seeing the same view I was seeing, as Myrrh progressed toward the chamber.

And there it was: a reasonably comfortable room with a bed, potty, dice and other games, a half-finished clay sculpture of a woman that looked rather like Jewel, two alert guards, and a sleeping boy. This was my first view of him. He was about eleven years old and fairly handsome.

What's his name? Myrrh's thought came.

Duban. That was Jewel's answer, which I heard as Myrrh's mind received it.

"Duban," Myrrh called softly.

The boy woke. "Who are you?" he demanded irritably.

"I am the girl you will marry," she said, still softly so that the guards would not overhear.

"When camels sprout wings," he said. "What have you brought me? More piss and dung from the battleaxe?"

Myrrh brought the platter up and set it on the foot of the bed. "This is your last meal."

"Very well. You delivered it. Not get your scrawny behind out of here."

"You won't find it scrawny when we marry. I am required to stay here and make sure you eat your meal, so you will be ready for the sacrifice."

Duban focused on her. "Why are you saying these things? You're just one more silly servant girl."

Myrrh leaned close to him. "Your mother sent me."

"You're not even a good liar! What does that female dog want with me, after deserting me for two years?"

"She didn't desert you. You were stolen from her, and she has not rested since. She has come to rescue you from the horror that awaits you." Myrrh glanced at the sculpture. "And you have not forgotten her."

"I've had enough of this nonsense." He turned his face toward the guards, about to summon them.

Myrrh caught his head between her hands and kissed him firmly on the mouth. It was a long kiss, and she must have augmented it with a thought, because when she let him go, he looked flushed and dazed.

The guards, seeing it happen, laughed. They evidently liked seeing a scullery maid tease the prisoner.

Soon Duban caught his breath. "Who are you?" he asked again, this time with genuine interest. Kisses could be potent persuaders, as I knew from Jewel.

Myrrh took his hand in hers. "I am Myrrh, your future wife. I can read minds. I know they plan to kill you tonight, a blood sacrifice for the ascension of the djinn Zeyn to mortal status so he can take over the throne. This is your last meal, and it is spiked with bhang. Don't eat anything but the yak cheese and chocolate."

"What do you know of yak cheese and chocolate?"

"You suspected their fell design. That's why you asked for those rare foods. Your mother got the chocolate with the help of the djinn of the lamp. Now you must come with us into the lamp, so you can escape the dread fate they plan for you."

Duban shook his head. "This is unbelievable, yet I am starting to believe you. But why do they want me dead? I am nobody important."

"You are to be the son of a king," she said persuasively. "And a great magician. I can feel that potential lurking in you. It needs only to be aroused and trained. They mean to kill you before that power manifests, so that there will be no possible competition for the usurper king."

"I'm no magician!"

"Not yet. But close. You must have felt it in you, like a rising tide. I can help you achieve it."

"I don't believe it!" Then he paused. "You are in my mind! Doing something! Like uncovering a buried chamber. But I don't want you messing in there. Stay out of my mind!"

Myrrh caught his face again and kissed him.

"You're a sorceress!" he said weakly.

"No. Only a girl who can read minds, and some of the future. Look into my mind." She continued holding his hand.

He gazed into her eyes. "I believe you," he said. "You say my mother sent you?"

"Yes. To rescue you. She is here, and will come to you soon. But you must allow me to help you, because there is powerful evil magic here."

"I—I—maybe I will. There is something about you."

"It is my burgeoning love for you, coloring my mind when I touch yours. Let me see if I can rouse your own magical powers."

"Yes," Duban agreed faintly. It was evident that he was beginning to feel some similar emotion toward her, and wanted to be close to her. The girl had learned well from Jewel about managing men.

"I think not."

Both children froze, then turned to face the new voice.

It was the djinn Zeyn, and he was glowering.

I reverted to my own awareness. We had to act immediately, or all was lost.

CHAPTER TWENTY-SEVEN

I rubbed my ring. "Faddy!"

There was no more hiding the fact we were here, and even if Zeyn had the ability to pinpoint the presence of another djinn, we would be on the move. At least, that was my plan, as feeble as it was.

A mist formed in front of me, and rapidly took on shape. My old friend and djinn appeared. He bowed slightly, although he had not fully materialized.

"I'll dispense with the pleasantries," said Faddy, "and tell you that you have just alerted Lord Zeyn of your exact location."

"Lord Zeyn is busy with Duban and Myrrh."

"Perhaps, master. But he is also a great magician, fully capable of wreaking havoc in more places than one. Rest assured he has already alerted Ibrahim's soldiers."

Ibrahim was, of course, Jewel's ex-husband. "I'm aware that there is great danger at every turn, Faddy, which is why I have summoned you."

"But my very presence is a beacon—"

"I am willing to take that chance. Find me the fastest and safest route to Jewel and the others."

He bowed and immediately disappeared. I hastily set aside the can of refuse and drew my scimitar, listening, certain I had heard boots running from one of the side tunnels. I started back the way I had come when a voice appeared in my ear.

"Not that way, master. Guards are coming. There is a side tunnel that will get you there, albeit quite a good deal longer."

I needed to get to Jewel and the others as soon as possible. "How many soldiers?"

"A half dozen. Too many for even you, master."

"Could you cause a distraction?"

"I can do whatever is ordered of me."

I shook my head angrily. Damn the ifrits and their literal translations. "Would a distraction work?"

"Hard to know, master. Sometimes you just have to try it and see."

Good point. Nothing is written in stone, and it was high time I started trusting my own instincts. "Mimic my voice and the sounds of running feet down a side tunnel. Even if only half peel off, I'll take my chances with three men."

Faddy bowed and departed and I continued down the tunnel. As I ran, I searched for the faint second sight Myrrh had provided me for my benefit, but the mirage-like image was gone. Evidently, Myrrh was not a great magician and was incapable of doing two things at once, like fending off Zeyn, and providing Jewel and me a glimpse into her mind.

I heard men shouting and the sound of boots running on stone. The sounds faded away, and as I turned a corner I was faced with two heavily armed men. I could handle two men.

Without hesitation or thought, I lunged forward, aiming the point of my scimitar for the nearest guard's throat. He parried, knocking my blade away…and directly into the chest of his fellow guard. The man screamed and dropped his weapon, grabbing at the blade. I kicked him away and pulled free the blood-soaked end of my sword. As I did so, the first guard was already swinging his own steel, I leaned back and took the point of his weapon across my cheek. Blood poured free and I knew the cut would be bad. For now, though, I could give a damn. Already leaning back, I dropped to a knee and thrust my own blade up hard. The equivalent of an uppercut. My sword struck home in his groin and carried up into his bowels and no doubt all the way to his heart. He was dead by the time I kicked him away and freed my blade.

I was running again down a lighted tunnel, the smell of blood already strong in the air. At another corner, I paused and listened. Already I was losing my bearings. There were shouts from somewhere, but nothing nearby. I wasn't worried about getting lost. Faddy had his purposes, and once such purpose was to be my eyes and ears. With Faddy around, I was never truly lost.

I reached back and pulled around the satchel I had been carrying. I opened it and withdrew the magical lamp. Three rubs later and black smoke poured from the small opening. The black smoke never fully took place. Lamprey didn't always take solid form and now that he was recovering the tortures he'd endured, it seemed less likely.

"I need your help, Lamprey."

"I imagine you do."

"Do you know the situation?"

"Have you forgotten that I was traveling along your back, master? I hear what you hear."

"Then you know that Zeyn is here."

"I would know that anyway. I feel him, as he now feels me. Even at this moment he is casting around, searching for me."

"Can you shield yourself somehow?"

"I already have, but my appearance alone has alerted him."

"Fine," I said. Somewhere someone screamed. It sounded like a girl. But it was impossible to tell with all these blasted tunnels. "How powerful is Zeyn?"

"One of the most powerful djinns."

"More powerful than you?"

"We have similar power, master. Except I am bound to you and he is bound to no one. Such freedom gives him more leverage, which is how he captured me."

"He answers to no one."

"Exactly. Whereas I must answer to you."

"Then I command you to stop him. I command you to kill him."

Now Lamprey solidified some more. The djinn, who was tall and gaunt, adopted a look of grave regret. "Perhaps if I was not weakened I could have carried out your command. Perhaps. With Zeyn there are no guarantees, as he is cunning and known for his use of powerful dark magicks."

"How is it that such a being is in our world?"

"He was summoned by Ibrahim. Djinns cannot voluntarily operate in the mortal realms without a host. Little does Ibrahim know the powerful forces he's dealing with."

"In essence, we have one of Djinnland's most powerful magicians loosed in our world."

"In essence. But his presence is still limited to Ibrahim's invocations."

"So, although he's not bound to Ibrahim, he can only manifest when invoked."

"True."

"Which is why he's seeking a mortal body."

"True again. With such a body, he will have free reign in your mortal realm, bound to no one, although he seeks to control you."

I already knew much of this, but it was nice knowing what I was fully up against. I thought hard, even as a another wavering scream echoed down the hallway. In that moment, Myrrh's second sight appeared in my thoughts, and I saw an image of Jewel being dragged off, bloodied and beaten. Myrrh and the boy were being led away, hauled along by brutish soldiers. Seeing Jewel bloodied and nearly unconscious—a mother fighting for the life of her child, and a woman I had come to have more feelings for than I ever thought possible—awakened a blinding rage within me. The image faded just as I saw Myrrh plunge through an arched opening…and into the main sanctuary. Men were everywhere, having formed a circle around a bloodied altar. Jewel fought again, and a man leveled a kick square into her side, sending her tumbling over the smooth stone floor.

And then the image wavered and disappeared. Myrrh had given me the best image she could, without her own fear and pain disrupting the transmission of it.

"Lamprey," I growled, fighting to control myself. "Can you at least slow Zeyn down?"

He hesitated, and even through my anger I sensed the reason for his reluctance. I sensed I was putting him at great risk, and possibly even exposing him to death. But he was bound to me, ordered to do my bidding.

"I can do my best, master."

"I do not want any harm to befall you, my friend," I said. "But I need your help. I must insist on it."

He seemed to take in some air, and then nodded. "Of course, master."

"Begone," I said. "And I wish you godspeed."

And with that he was gone. I next ordered Faddy to guide me through the tunnels, and he did just that. Shortly, I was standing just inside a smaller archway, looking out into the main sanctuary. And what I saw made my blood boil.

The boy was being forced onto an altar, while an immaculately groomed man in an ornate robe watched icily from a raised stone platform. Ibrahim, I assumed. The boy's own father. Jewel was on her knees nearby, bleeding and weeping, held down by two guards. She struggled against them, and I knew it was only a matter of time before they silenced her with a quick blade across her throat. Myrrh was nearby as well, restrained by a guard who had a fistful of her hair. And standing in the shadows behind Ibrahim was a massive figure. A figure who was looking increasingly pleased. It was Zeyn.

Where Lamprey had gone, I didn't know. But I had just decided to blindly rush to the boy's aid, when words appeared in mind.

Patience, my liege.

It was Myrrh.

I am out of patience, I thought desperately, *and the boy has no time.*

Your djinn is near.

As they began to strap the boy down and as Jewel let out a great wail, something caught my eye. Smoke from the torches seemed to be congealing in the air above the proceedings. Indeed, what had once been wispy black smoke now took on the shape of a man. No, not a man.

Lamprey.

No one seemed to notice. No one, that is, except for Zeyn. The massive djinn stepped out of the shadows, looking up.

I looked up, too, and saw that the image of Lamprey was gone, having been replaced by a swirling vortex of black smoke. The smoke soon took on another shape. A much larger and far different shape.

A moment later, a black dragon bellowed loudly, blasting fire, and all hell broke loose.

CHAPTER TWENTY-EIGHT

The sight of the black dragon terrified the assembled spectators, who fled madly toward the main exit, trampling each other. But the guards, more disciplined, held their positions. Realizing that they could not get out, the throng of people paused restlessly.

Zeyn glanced around, then beckoned Ibrahim, Jewel's ex, and Duban's father. The man came forward immediately.

The guards continued to push the boy to the altar. "Father!" he cried as Ibrahim approached. "Save me!"

"Prepare him," Ibrahim said curtly to the guards.

"Father!" the boy repeated. "Don't let them do this to me!"

"Stop being a brat and get on that altar," the man snapped.

"Father!" Duban cried a third time. "Don't you understand? They mean to kill me!"

So he was starting to see the light, thanks to what Myrrh had told him.

"It's the necessary ritual sacrifice. We've been preparing for this event for years. Why do you think I brought you here? It's a rare honor for you."

The boy looked at his father with horror, crushed by this betrayal. He stopped resisting the guards as they tied him down on the altar.

Myrrh's thought came: *He thought his father loved him.*

Meanwhile Zeyn was dissolving into smoke, which formed into another dragon. This one was bright red, with fire not only on its breath, but radiating from its torso and tail. It looked healthier than the black dragon, unfortunately.

I remained where I was, as no one had noticed me yet, and the sacrifice seemed not to be immediate. If Lamprey defeated Zeyn, that would change the picture. If not, I would make a desperate effort to save Duban from the knife.

The two dragons circled each other in the air. The chamber was so big that there was room for even such huge flying creatures to maneuver. The people below, realizing that the dragons were not hunting them, gazed up, watching. This was a spectacle seldom seen by mortals.

The black dragon lunged, sending a blast of fire at the red dragon's tail. But the other whipped the tail clear, and sent a blast of its own that just missed Lamprey's head. Stroke and counter-stroke, and the advantage seemed to be with Zeyn.

Now the red dragon fired another blast at Lamprey's head. That seemed to be a tactical error, as Lamprey readily whipped his head out of the way. But then the red dragon shot forward, its jaws snapping at the black dragon's momentarily exposed neck. I realized two things: this was a contest of maneuvering more than one of fire, with the more adroit tactician gaining the advantage, such as singeing the other. And that Zeyn had set up a two strike combination, with first the fire to make Lamprey react, then the teeth to catch him when he did. A chomp on the neck could sever vital nerves and finish the fight immediately.

But Lamprey was evidently no amateur in such duels. Not only did his neck avoid the closing jaws, the tip of his tail snapped forward with a whip-like crack across the red snout, just missing an eye. Lamprey had his own combinations. Had that whip scored, Zeyn would have been half blinded.

After that the red dragon was more cautious about fancy ploys, being evidently outmatched in that respect. It was looking better for Lamprey. So why had he hesitated about getting into this duel?

Then I saw that he was slowing. At full strength he might be the superior dragon, but he had been weakened, and now was running out of energy. Zeyn's attacks were getting stronger, while Lamprey's defenses were getting weaker. It was not after all a fair fight.

Now the red dragon made an all-out charge with fire and teeth. The black dragon could not fend it off. He would soon be vanquished, and then dead. *Escape!* I thought to him, knowing he remained attuned to my commands. *Hide! Get out of here and save your hide any way you can!*

Defeated, Lamprey turned tail literally and fled. He flew down the main passage and out the front gate, crashing through the barriers, the red dragon hot in pursuit. It was an ignominious rout. No one else knew that it was not fear, but my order, that brought it on.

The red dragon pursued the black dragon on out of the temple. The audience relaxed, for being this close to battling dragons was not the safest situation. Any missed blast of fire or falling body could wipe out many people.

It was not enough time, Myrrh's thought came. *Duban's magician power is looming close, but he must rouse it himself. He isn't trying. He doesn't believe me and doesn't care.*

The guards were completing the tie-down of the sacrificial boy. "Resist!" Jewel called to him. "Fight them! Get off the altar!"

"Kill her!" Ibrahim screamed. One guard lifted his scimitar.

"No!" Duban cried, lifting his head so he could see her. "She's my mother!" He might not think much of her, but he knew she did not deserve death.

Ibrahim's lip curled. "She's a has-been slut."

Duban's angry, knowing it's a slur, but it's not enough.

Two guards hauled the struggling Jewel to her feet and held her helpless for the attack by the third. It occurred to me that it must have been much the same way when the other guards raped her. No one or two men could have handled her, but three was too much for her to resist.

Suddenly I was in motion, heedless of the bleeding wound on my head. I charged across the hall to Jewel, swinging my own scimitar. I lopped off the head of the armed guard before he even saw me, and turned on the other. He was just drawing his weapon when I cut off his sword arm. He abruptly lost interest in combat. The third, coward that he was, was hastily backing off.

But now Ibrahim was striding across, drawing his own scimitar. "Beware!" Jewel hissed. "He's an expert!"

Oh, was he? Then this should be fun. I whirled on him, my blade swinging viciously. I wanted to end it with the first cut.

I'm telling Duban that you are the king, come to rescue him and marry his mother. He accepts that, but doesn't care.

Ibrahim met me coolly, effortlessly turning aside my blade. He was indeed expert. We fenced, and soon I recognized his style. He had been taught by a master. But like all styles, it had its liabilities. Few would ever live long enough to discover them, but I had been taught by a better master and already knew them.

Yet Duban, knowing now what his father did, hopes he'll lose. The anger he felt when he thought his mother deserted him has transferred to his father, the true betrayer.

I fenced imperfectly, seeming to be not Ibrahim's equal in skill. My ragged clothing and blood-soaked face surely contributed to the impression. He recognized his supposed superiority, and another sneer curled his lip. He thought he had an easy victory. Overconfidence can be deadly, especially when not justified. I made an error of form, laying myself open to the most devastating cut in the arsenal, and of course he took it, not even thinking about it; it was an automatic response. That was both an asset and liability: asset when speed counted most, liability when it was a trap.

You are not impressing Duban.

I lurched away, barely avoiding the slash, my weapon dropping low. He strode after me, eager to finish it. And the curve of my scimitar came up between his legs, hard, slicing into his groin from below.

He stood there a moment before he realized that he was finished. He had fallen for the ancient defeated-duffer ruse and was done for. Then he realized, and collapsed in blood. He would be dead before any surgeon could help.

"Good show!" Jewel cried. But more guards were converging. More than I could handle.

Then the red dragon returned, snorting fire. It was evident from his annoyance that he had not nailed his opponent, but lost him in the great outdoors. Probably Lamprey had changed form to an invisible gnat or desert toad and escaped detection. I was relieved.

The dragon dissolved into smoke, which coalesced into the djinn Zeyn. "Do not harm the man," he said. "Immobilize him. He is King Aladdin, to be my puppet ruler after this night, lending legitimacy to my assumption of power."

Duban doesn't like that. He thought you were a good king.

Well, bless the boy! I was beginning to like him.

Guards piled on me. I did not resist, as it would be impossible to overwhelm them all; I needed to wait for a better time.

"What of the woman?" a guard asked.

"Save her too. She may become my puppet queen. Ibrahim had abysmal judgment in most things, but had a flash of taste when he married her. Then he reverted to form, and dumped her for a younger tease. She should make a fine bedmate, for a while, once she has been declawed."

Duban really *doesn't like that. Now he knows his mother was the one who truly loved him.*

Guards surrounded Jewel, and she submitted, guided by my example. She had been picking up Myrrh's thoughts too.

"She's my mother!" Duban protested.

"Fancy that." Zeyn returned to the alter and drew the sacrificial knife. "Do you have any other foolish last words before I send you to Hades?"

Now Jewel struggled, but to no avail.

Myrrh, I thought. *What do you have for us?*

I am still trying to evoke Duban's magic, but he doesn't believe in it. He is also still a bit ambivalent about his mother. He feels betrayed and defeated; I can't evoke his deeper passion.

Passion will do it?

Maybe. That or outrage. It's the only chance.

Zeyn was lifting the knife, intoning the ritual for sacrifice. Duban was not trying to protest any more.

I suffered a flash of genius. *Connect Duban to Jewel's mind.*

Why? He doesn't fully believe she loves him. After his father's betrayal, he hesitates to believe anyone can truly be trusted, regardless what they say.

Just do it. Now!

Zeyn continued the ritual. There was very little time left.

I became aware of the hall as seen through Jewel's eyes. I saw Duban look up, surprised. The connection had been made.

"Jewel," I called. "How do you feel about your son?"

Her surge of feeling was answer enough. "I love him." That could no longer be doubted, because it was direct emotion. Now Duban knew.

That set up the real question. "What happened when Ibrahim's men first took you captive?"

She did not answer; it was not something she cared to share with others. But her mind could not help focusing on it now that I had reminded her. Suddenly I saw her terrible memory, of being held by two guards while the third ripped away her clothing, then his own, revealing his hard erection. She screamed and fought, but they held her secure while he came at her and violently raped her. The outrage and pain of the violation suffused the memory of it. That was just the first rape, followed immediately by others as the guards swapped places, each hornier than the last, turned on as much by what they were seeing as by their own lust. I saw and felt it, for the connection included her savage emotion. No wonder she had later gutted those criminals!

And her son Duban saw and felt it all, in cruelly unsparing detail.

So close! Now he understands completely, and is outraged. His power is rising.

But was there time?

Zeyn finished his intonation and brought the knife to Duban's throat.

There was what felt like an explosion. Zeyn, closest to the boy, was blown away, stunned. He landed on the floor on his back.

Duban sat up and flexed his arms. The stout cords binding him snapped. He flung out one arm in a theatrical gesture. There was a blinding flash of sheer power. The guards holding me and Jewel fell down as if clubbed, but we were untouched. This was magic indeed!

The boy ran to his mother, crying. She put her arms about him and held him close. He had erupted in outrage and found his power, but for the moment he was just a boy again.

That did it, Myrrh thought, satisfied.

The new Magician had finally been evoked.

CHAPTER TWENTY-NINE

I looked to where Zeyn had fallen, but the djinn was no where to be found. Had he died? Or had he departed back to Djinnland? I secretly hoped the foul djinn was meeting his maker; after all, djinns, like mankind, must account for their actions before Allah.

Seeing the ferocious power of the boy, I could see why Zeyn had sought to destroy him. And the djinn would have succeeded if not for the girl.

Sword in hand, I stepped over the fallen guards, most of whom still appeared to be alive. As I strode over to Jewel and Duban, I caught sight of many confused and shocked faces huddled along the far walls. Surely most of them had thought they were here only for their filthy blood ceremony, not the supernatural spectacle they had witnessed.

Myrrh broke free from the guard and dashed over to Jewel and Duban. As Jewel reached out and hugged the young girl, I soon found myself standing in the center of the chamber. Here, just moments earlier, two dragons had battled high in the air above. A sight I would not soon forget.

I paused in this sanctuary, not two feet from the altar where the boy's blood would surely have been spilled in the name of some arcane dark god. What entity could bestow a physical body to Zeyn, I did not know, and I hoped I would never find out.

I had everyone's attention, from Jewel and the kids, to the guards and the other attendees. A dark alliance was to be forged here tonight, of that I had no doubt, with Zeyn having designs to rule all. Everyone here had come to witness a human sacrifice, and for that my blood boiled.

Not everyone, my liege, came Myrrh's words into my mind. *As I scan their thoughts, there are some here who did not know what they were getting themselves into.*

I nodded, suddenly aware that many had been duped tonight. Zeyn was a cunning enemy. He had successfully used Ibrahim's influence to orchestrate tonight's events. But little did Ibrahim know that Zeyn had no use for him and would have disposed of him if all had gone according to plan.

And he would have disposed of one other, my lord. King Huran is here himself.

Oh? I thought, suddenly very curious; after all, Huran had been my first in command, and I had known him to be a fair and just man, which is why I had entrusted my kingdom to him.

He still is, my lord. The king is being held prisoner very near where we found my future husband. In fact, King Huran is unaware of the recent events and is certain he is next to be sacrificed.

I rubbed my ring.

"Master?" Faddy words appeared instantly in my ear.

"King Huran is being held prisoner here," I said quietly, sub-vocalizing my words. "Find him, free him, and bring him to me."

"As you wish, master."

With Faddy gone, I spun my sword once, twice, letting the torchlight play on its smooth, blood-stained surface. I turned in a small circle and took in the entire room. All eyes were on me; something I was accustomed to. I noticed some edging toward the exits, the guards included. The night, obviously, had not gone as planned.

"No one leaves," I said loudly, my voice reverberating in the cavernous room. "Unless you wish to meet my dragon again."

That stopped them. I wasn't sure what was going to happen, but before anything did, I wanted King Huran by my side. I caught Jewel's eye as she held her son close. Tears streamed down her face and I did not blame her. Her love for her son reminded me of my own loss, but I fought back my own pain.

He's coming now, reported Myrrh.

Indeed, I could hear the echoing of running feet and a moment later my good friend and confidant appeared in the sanctuary. He blinked hard, taking in the scene. He looked the worse for wear; indeed, he too had suffered torture of one sort or another. He was bloodied and dressed in ragged clothing. Those standing in the shadows recognized him immediately. After all, he had been their king for many years while I had been in my self-exile. A murmur arose and then heads began to bow. Confused, Huran continued to scan the crowd. Surely he thought this was a prank, perhaps a final humiliation before he was sacrificed alongside the boy.

And then he spotted me. "Aladdin?" he asked, his voice weak.

"The one and only, my good friend."

We moved toward each other and embraced warmly, aware that all eyes were still on us. Also from the shadows I saw another man moving, Sa'ood. I nodded toward him and he immediately dashed over to his daughter and hugged her tightly.

"They were going to kill me," said Huran. "I presume you saved my hide."

"Again," I said.

He laughed, but there was little humor in the sound. I could only imagine what he must have endured as a prisoner. He continued scanning the crowd. "I recognize many," he said. "Traitors, I presume."

"Again, you presume correctly. Some, but not all."

"So what is stopping them from killing us now?" asked the reigning king.

"They fear you and me...and perhaps some of the friends I brought along."

"But I see no friends."

"Ah, and those are scariest of all."

"You speak in riddles, Aladdin."

"I will explain all soon enough," I said. "But, for now, we have work to do."

"No, my old friend. *I* do not have work to do. *You* have work to do."

"I do not understand...."

"Then let me spell it out for you, *King* Aladdin. I've had enough of the job. The petty quarreling, the court politics, the backstabbing, the intrigue, the pomp and circumstance, the lies and jealousy."

"Do not make it sound so glamorous," I said, laughing lightly, although my eyes continued scanning the mostly submissive crowd.

"I am a warrior, Aladdin. A general. I long for the battlefield, not the ballrooms. I long to hold cold steel in my hand, not the proper silver spoon."

I chuckled lightly, but now looked my friend straight in the eye. "What are you saying?"

"I am saying you can have your job back."

And what King Huran did next surprised even me. He took my left hand in both of his and dropped to a knee, bowing his head, the common gesture of allegiance. There were more murmurings from those standing in the shadows. King Huran stood, clapped me on the shoulder and raised his voice loudly.

"Many of you would do well never to return to Agrabah, for you will surely meet a long and unfortunate end. I do not take kindly to traitors...nor does King Aladdin." He paused, letting his words sink in, perhaps as much for my benefit as for any other. "Yes, King Aladdin is back, and pray to Allah for your souls."

I was stunned. Too stunned for words. Not just two days ago I had been living contentedly in my simple tent, often moving from dusty village to village, taking on odd jobs and doing my best to forget the pain in my heart. But little had I known a plot had been conspired from afar, in lands I had only dreamed of, by beings I had not fully understood or cared to know. I had sworn off the throne, determined to live a simple life.

I glanced sharply to my left, catching movement. Jewel was walking slowly toward me, regal and beautiful despite her battering, her arm draped over the shoulders of her weeping boy, a boy who could not pull his eyes off his recently killed father. A man killed by my own hands.

Jewel. So beautiful. So determined. So passionate. She reminded me to live and to love, and had awakened in me something I had long ago thought I had lost forever.

She continued over to my side and slipped her hand in my hand. The gesture was simple but meaningful. She was mine and I was hers. Huran smiled at her and stepped away, bowing.

I had not sought to be king again, but the kingdom was mine. Again.

As I said, my liege, came Myrrh's soft words in my head. *Tonight, a ruler will be named and a great magician revealed.*

No one likes a know-it-all, I thought, and grinned. *Now begone from my thoughts, lass.*

As you wish, King Aladdin.

And I felt a noticeable presence leave my forethoughts. The girl was indeed a powerful sorceress. She and the boy would make a formidable team—and a valuable aid to any ruler.

I took in a lot of air and surveyed the small group around me. I had been alone for so long, a lonely adventurer grieving for what had been lost. And now so much had been returned.

My scanning eyes settled on a dark-clad, hooded figure watching us from the shadows of one of the tunnels. A chill ran through me, for I knew I had seen Death. The man—or creature—turned and disappeared into the shadows.

Death had indeed made an appearance tonight, but not for me, and not for those I had already come to love.

A few choice words later and those who had proved to be less than faithful scuttled out of the great temple like the dung beetles they were. Each of their faces were forever seared into my memory, should any one of them return to my kingdom.

Now we were grouped outside the awesome temple as sunlight appeared in the east, rising over the lip of the canyon walls. It had been a long night. Medics had staunched the flow of blood on my face and made me look halfway presentable, servants had washed off the taint of the garbage I had handled and gotten me fresh clothing, and I felt much better.

I had summoned Lamprey and soon discovered that the powerful ifrit, although heavily weakened and badly wounded, had indeed survived. Apparently, he had changed form into a black ant, safe under a rock until I had summoned him again. Now he was resting comfortably in his lamp, which was strapped securely to my riding horse. He assured us that he did not have the strength to transport us all back to Agrabah, my kingdom.

Just as well, I thought, there were a few of us eager to get to know each other a little better.

And court politics could always wait.

As we headed out into the rising sun, kicking up dust and riding steadily, General Huran rode over to my side, nodding to Jewel who had been riding next to me. Young Duban was sitting in front of her. I did not think Jewel would let the lad out of her sight ever again.

"My liege," said Huran. "Prior to my getting falsely arrested and kidnapped, a curious sailor appeared before me."

"Who was this sailor?"

"He called himself Sinbad and he was seeking sponsorship for a voyage."

"A voyage where?"

"To a strange island inhabited by rocs and cyclops and mountains of gold."

I laughed heartily. "Allah bless the dreamers! And what did you tell him?"

"I told him I would get back to him."

I laughed again. "Then surely he is still waiting. Perhaps I will speak to this Sinbad."

"As you wish, sire."

Huran slipped away again and Jewel closed in next to me. She reached out a hand, and I reached out mine, and we rode like that into the morning sun.

THE END

To be continued in:

ALADDIN SINS BAD

The Aladdin Trilogy #2

Available now!
Kindle * Kobo * Nook
Amazon UK * Apple * Smashwords
Paperback * Audio Book

Also available:

REALTY CHECK

by Piers Anthony

Realty Check is available at:
Kindle * Kobo * Nook
Amazon UK * Apple * Paperback

CHAPTER ONE

"Remember, the Realtor warned us the key card can be used only once," Chandelle reminded him. "Don't let that door close before we're inside." They had been married forty years, but she still felt compelled to remind him of details.

"Got it," Penn agreed. The door opened, and they stepped into the house.

It was beautiful. They stood in the living room, gazing at the carpeted floor, the picture window at the side, the couch, chairs, and the large television set. "It's really furnished!" she exclaimed, surprised. Penn nodded. "The ad did say it was. But I assumed it would be token, or junky. This is all new."

"I hope we can afford it." She paused, then added: "Assuming we want it." But the truth was that she liked it already. It was in the right location and the neighborhood was good. Unless there was something drastically wrong with the house, it would do for their summer.

"The ad said one month's rent free," he reminded her. "If the second month turns out to be exorbitant, we can move out. I wonder why the other prospects turned it down? It couldn't have been the price, if they didn't even know it."

"Even if the price was too high, that free month should have made them stay that long," she agreed. "And why wouldn't Ms. Dunbar come with us?" he asked rhetorically. "Realtors always show the houses. They want to clinch the sale."

"She said the proprietor left strict orders," Chandelle said. "Prospects have to look at it alone. Maybe the owner doesn't want any sales pressure."

"You know what? We're stalling. We're afraid something's wrong with it, so we're standing here telling each other what we already know, instead of checking out the house."

She nodded. "Yes we are. We had better go ahead and discover the reason this remains open, so at least we'll know."

They moved through the living room to the adjacent small dining room, and the kitchen beyond. Chandelle stood in the center and turned slowly around, while Penn opened the door to the garage and went in. "Hey, there are tools here—and bicycles," he exclaimed. "Mountain bikes. The prior renter didn't clean out all his stuff."

"There was no prior renter, dear," she said, reminding him again. "Nobody wanted to rent."

"Then the owner is storing stuff here," he muttered.

Was he? Chandelle checked under the gleaming kitchen sink. Sure enough, it was equipped with a quality garbage disposal unit. She pulled open a drawer. There was silverware in it, neatly sorted, of good quality. She opened a cupboard. There were assorted canned goods. She went to the freezer. It was well stocked with frozen foods. She recognized the brand names: all top quality, the kind she favored. All unused, with current "sell-by" dates. This could not be an accident. "The rent must be astronomical," she breathed. "If all this is part of the furnishings."

Penn came back into the kitchen, shaking his head. "Those tools have not been used. It's as if the owner set it up to please himself, then changed his mind. And those bikes—brand new, lightweight, in perfect working order. Not cheap equipment. He couldn't have forgotten those."

"The kitchen is completely stocked," she said. "Food included. Even a furnished house does not include that."

"With food?" He opened the refrigerator door. There was a jug of milk, a can of fruit juice, a head of lettuce, packages of cheese, and assorted other items. "We could make sandwiches right here. This has all the makings I like."

"Yes, there's a loaf of bread in the breadbox," she agreed. "Fresh today, and the kind we prefer. So we know it isn't accidental. The owner must really want to rent this house."

"Maybe when the others turned it down, he decided to make it more appealing. But it's a nice enough house regardless. Why would anybody turn it down, without even taking the free month?"

They kept coming back to that. She was as mystified as he. She went to the stairway to check the bedrooms, while he went out the back door.

She paused at the base of the stairway. There was a small picture, or plaque, on the wall there. On it was inscribed a simple circle. Did it have a purpose? She would have to call it to Penn's attention. She went on up the stairs.

She was hardly surprised to find the master bedroom set up, its bed neatly made, the top sheet turned in the manner of a hotel room setup. She checked the closets: sure enough, there were suits in one, dresses in the other. There was linen in the linen closet, and socks and underwear in drawers.

On an idle fancy, she took down a hanging dress and tried it on over her own. It fit her almost perfectly. She tied the sash and buttoned the blouse, then tugged the hem straight. She walked to the master bathroom and looked in its wall-sized mirror. Yes, were it not for the slight lumpiness occasioned by the clothing beneath, this would be a perfectly useful and attractive dress. Certainly as good as the rack items she normally bought.

She returned to the closet and looked below. There were shoes: men's under the suits, ladies' under the dresses. Could they possibly fit? They looked as if they might. Yet shoe sizing was a personal thing; every foot was different. A perfect fit was unlikely to be by chance.

This was getting scary. Coincidence could hardly account for it. Someone wanted the two of them here. She was beginning to appreciate why the other prospects had been scared away. This was too much like the spider inviting the fly into its parlor.

Then she became aware of a noise. It was a measured beating or pounding, as in someone banging against a wall.

Suddenly she was frightened. Penn! Where was he?

She ran down the stairs to the kitchen. The sound was coming from the back door. She hurried to open it. There stood Penn, looking abashed. "Honey, come out here a moment," he said. "But prop open that door."

"Whatever for? We don't want to let the bugs in. And why didn't you just come back in yourself? Did the door lock?"

"Not exactly. Just come out."

She hauled a kitchen chair across and propped the door open. Then she stepped outside. And stood amazed. She faced what looked like an endless forest. Large old trees were everywhere, extending as far as she could see. "But this is in the middle of the city," she protested somewhat inanely. "The back yard can't be this big!"

"Now turn around," he said tightly.

Obediently, she turned. And gasped. The house was gone. There was only a boulder there—with the propped-open door in it. Beyond it she could see the forest, extending endlessly, in all directions.

"I walked all the way around that rock," Penn said. "There's nothing but forest here."

"But—but it's a two story house. It can't possibly fit inside that stone. And the city—where's the city?"

"Now we know why the other prospects turned it down," he said. "I'm just glad I had the wit to pound on that rock."

"I'm glad too," she said weakly. "Penn, there is something very strange here."

He made a droll face. "You're telling me?"

"Upstairs, the bed's made. There is linen, and clothing. In fact—" She paused, realizing that she was still wearing the dress she had been trying on. "There is clothing. I tried on a dress."

"And it fits," he said, recognizing the unfamiliarity of the outfit.

"Maybe we should go in and try on the shoes," she said.

"Maybe we should." For he knew as well as she did that shoes were highly individual.

They entered the boulder, which was the house, inside. Penn paused to poke his head back out, while holding one hand up inside, verifying that the house was larger inside than out. "I can see out," he reported, "but not in. There's no window on the outside." He wiggled his fingers inside. Then he reversed, looking out the door window while wiggling his fingers outside. They showed clearly. He shook his head, bemused.

Chandelle knew Penn would never rest until he fathomed that mystery, as well as that of the forest itself. But right now he was working on her mystery, and in a moment he moved clear, removed the chair, and carefully closed the door.

They went upstairs to the bedroom. Then she took a pair of lady shoes, and he took a pair of man shoes, and they sat beside each other on the bed and tried them on.

They fit. Chandelle didn't know whether to feel satisfied or alarmed. "How can this be?"

"It is possible," Penn said. "Maybe we were targeted. Maybe they wanted healthy uncommitted retirees in their sixties. We made an appointment to come today. These days nothing is truly private. They could have known our sizes. Is that alarming?"

"Is it?" She wanted the reassurance of his logic.

He nodded. "Yes, I think it is. I would rather be anonymous, until I know what's going on. It is evident that I'm not. Have we plumbed the depth of the strangeness of this site, or is there more we need to know?"

"If it's a spider luring a fly, would it show the fly the strangeness?"

Penn put the shoes carefully back in their places. "This seems entirely too elaborate for anything inimical. Why didn't the spider simply grab the other prospects before they could leave?"

"Because the Realtor would know, and stop showing the house." Still, she was allowing herself to be reassured.

"I think it's selective, but not inimical," he said. "The proprietor is looking for folk who find a house like this appealing." He glanced at her. "Do we find it appealing?"

She considered. "The layout is nice. The facilities are nice. The location is ideal. Yes, it is appealing. But it scares me."

"Maybe it's supposed to."

"Supposed to?"

Penn spread his hands in the way he had, to indicate the shaping of a concept. "Suppose, for the sake of argument, that the proprietor wants a certain type of occupant. One canny enough to recognize the oddity of the site, and nervy enough to use it. So stupid or timid applicants need not apply."

"Then he wants you and not me," Chandelle said with a forced shudder.

"I don't think so. There's the house and the yard. That forest scares me, because I know it's impossible, but fascinates me for the same reason. Just as you caught on to the targeting of the food and clothing, which frighten yet intrigue you. He wants you too."

"But the house is ordinary. Scary only because of all the things it provides that Scrooge never offers. It's that forest that's impossible."

Penn reconsidered. "Well, maybe it wants folk who feel challenged by the impossible. But I won't stay without you. So the house has to make things nice for you, too."

Now Chandelle reconsidered. "Suppose the house is just as strange as the yard? Only we haven't seen the impossible aspect yet?"

"Then we'd better find out. We don't want to make a mistake either way."

They went downstairs and poked around more thoroughly. There was a den with a computer, so Penn turned it on. Chandelle watched over his shoulder. She had never quite gotten the hang of computers. In a moment the screen lighted, with a printed message. PLEASE SELECT DESIRED OPTION. Below was a list of programs, some of which she recognized. "This is pretty fancy," Penn said. "It seems to have a choice of about six operating systems, and it's very fast." He chose one, and it took over the screen.

She didn't inquire how he knew its speed. "Can it do letters?"

"Oh, yes. And it can surf the Internet. And more. This is too big for us; we need a teenager."

"Well, we will have one to entertain. Would this hold Llynn?" For Llynn was their elder granddaughter. They had come to this city in order to be near enough to take her off her family's hands for a while, because she was a handful at fifteen.

"It might, for a while. But I think she's more of a video freak."

"Next stop," she said, smiling. He shut down the computer. They went to the living room, where she turned on the TV set. It came on to a local station. She found the remote control and flicked through the channels. They were endless, and all were quite clear. This must be on a superior cable or satellite service. Some were even foreign language. "Couch potatoes and wild teens will love this," she said, turning it off.

Now she noticed that there were book shelves lining the walls. She went to look at the books, and saw that a number of her favorite titles were there. She saw a sound system, with a small library of compact disc albums. Some of her favorite music was there. There were pictures around the room. All of them appealed to her taste. "This proprietor is good," she murmured. "He has done his homework." But this, too, sent a quiet chill through her. Why should anyone study them so carefully, and offer such a phenomenal house, free?

Penn examined the window. It showed a scene of a weird alien landscape. "This is odd," he murmured. As if they hadn't encountered oddity enough already! She joined him. "It must be a painting behind glass. A true window would look out on the dull wall of the adjacent building. And no window on Earth would look out on a scene like that."

"But this one does. Try moving back and forth, and you'll see the perspective shift."

"They have three dimensional pictures now, holographs, that show perspective."

"I don't think this is a holograph." He went and rummaged in the garage. He returned in a moment with a long flashlight. He shone it through the window. The light passed through the glass and splashed across the sill, touching the dark earth beyond. A spaghetti shaped plant turned several strands to catch the light better. "Point made," she said. "That thing is alive and aware."

"And it doesn't grow on this world, I think."

She felt a chill. "I agree. I think the window is sealed because the air out there isn't breathable. Not by us."

"Not by us," he agreed. "It must be a special animation, but a sophisticated one." He gazed at it a moment more, then glanced down. "What's this?" He indicated a panel beside the window.

"Air conditioning control?" But it didn't look like it. It had numbers 1 through 0, and a bar. A tiny screen showed the number 14.

He touched the key labeled #1. Nothing happened. Then he touched the ACTIVATE bar below. The number changed to 1. The window scene changed. Now it was a dark sky filled with stars. In the foreground was a great moon. It wasn't Earth's moon.

They stood and gazed out, awed by the depth and power of the scene. "I don't recognize those constellations," Penn said.

"That moon is moving against the stellar background," Chandelle pointed out. "This is either a remarkable animation, or another actual scene."

"Maybe it's more cable TV. But then, how to explain that plant we just saw react?"

"Try another setting."

He touched #2, and the bar. A seascape appeared, with the waves surging across the rocks in the foreground. One large wave came, and its spume spattered against the window and slid down.

"This is something I shall want to explore farther," Penn said. He touched #1 and #4, and the bar, returning the scene to the original setting.

"Should we try the other panels?" she asked.

"Other panels?"

"The one beside the back door. And the front door."

"I hadn't noticed." He walked to the back, and she followed. There was the panel she had seen. It was set at #6.

Penn touched #7 and the bar. The forest changed. It had been large oak trees; now it was large pines.

"I've just got to check that," he said.

"I will guard the door. Don't go out of sight."

He opened the door and stepped out. She watched him go to the nearest pine tree. He reached out and touched it. But she already knew it was real, for the faint pleasant scent of pine sap and rotting needles wafted in. This was the confirmation that the scene really had changed. It wasn't just an illusion.

She saw Penn try to rip off a piece of bark, but it resisted his effort. So he bent to pick up some fallen needles, and came up with nothing. Why was that? He found a low twig and tried to pull some live needles from it, but couldn't. He turned and walked back to the house, a thoughtful expression on his face.

"I can't budge anything," he said as he entered. "I can see it, feel it, smell it, but not affect it. I almost thought that pine bough was swaying slightly in the wind, but I couldn't move it at all. Not half an iota."

"I saw. It's as if you aren't really there."

He laughed. "It's there, for sure! But I'm not. I'm a ghost." He turned to the panel, and moved it to #8. This time the forest seemed to be formed of giant ferns, each the size of a tree. He shook his head and touched #9. The landscape became barren rock, with an ugly mountain in the background. #10 brought a scene that looked like molten lava.

"Turn it back!" Chandelle said, alarmed.

He hastily touched #4 and hit the bar. That was a modern city scene.

"You got the wrong number," Chandelle said nervously. But now she wasn't quite sure which was the right one.

He tried #5. That was an ugly plain of brush and tree stumps. He touched #6, and the oak trees returned. They stared at each other. "This is really strange," Penn said.

Chandelle didn't care to advertise how foolishly alarmed she had been when they almost lost the original setting. "We had better try the front door knob," she said tightly.

He tilted his head. "Are you sure you're up to it, dear?"

"I don't dare avoid it. If the front changes too—" She shook her head, not finishing. This nice house had become frighteningly complicated.

They went to the front. That number was #73. Penn reached slowly for the panel, visibly set himself, and reset it to #74. They peered out the pane.

The city had changed. It remained a metropolis, but the street and buildings across it were different.

"More?" Penn asked.

"Turn it back."

He touched #73, and the familiar street returned. He withdrew from the panel as if it had become hot. They retreated to the living room couch and sat down. Penn put his arm around her back, and Chandelle put her head into his shoulder and cried. It was her way of handling extraordinary tension.

After a bit she disengaged. She had recovered some of her equilibrium. She dug into her purse for a hanky and patted her face. "What do you think it is?"

"Something well beyond anything we know." He looked shaken. "So maybe those are all images outside, with enough play to really seem real. But I don't think so. I think they're real. Which means this house is something really special. Whoever built it has technology we've never seen."

"But why?" she asked plaintively. "Why do all this, and just set it out for rent?"

"I'd sure like to know. Oh, would I like to know!"

She nerved herself, and spoke. "There's only one way to find out."

He nodded. "Rent it."

"Do you want to?"

"Honey, I don't want to upset you—"

"You want to rent it. Because we had a deal: one month in the city, with its culture, the way I like it, and then a month in the wilderness, roughing it, the way you've always dreamed. That's all available right here, depending on the door we use. And we have undertaken to take Llynn off her family's hands for a while. I think this house will interest her, and that's two thirds of the battle. Maybe she'll forget to be so wild."

"Yes. I have the feeling that everything we have known in life so far pales into insignificance beside this. We are being offered a chance to explore—to investigate, perhaps, the universe." He looked at her, the doubt manifest. "But do you really want to?"

She took a deep breath. "Definitely. Remember, my name means 'Candle.' It is better to light it, than to curse the darkness."

He kissed her. "I can't say you won't regret this."

"I know. But I'm curious too. And the first month's rate is right." She got up and walked to the phone. As she brought the receiver to her ear, she heard the beeping of automatic dialing. A programmed phone?

"Dunbar Reality, Karen speaking." It was their Realtor.

"Chandelle Green here. We're at the house. We want to rent."

"Excellent. I was afraid you wouldn't. But do you mind telling me—"

Chandelle avoided that by interrupting her. "This house has everything! The owner forgot to remove—"

"No. It is stocked for your convenience. Everything there is for you to use. Come to the office and we'll give you the permanent key."

"Thank you," Chandelle said faintly. "We'll be right there." She hung up the phone. "It's done. We just have to pick up the regular key. And we can use everything."

Also available:

MOON DANCE

Vampire for Hire #1

by J.R. Rain

Moon Dance is available at:
Kindle * Kobo * Nook
Amazon UK * Apple * Smashwords
Paperback * Audio Book

CHAPTER ONE

I was folding laundry in the dark and watching Judge Judy rip this guy a new asshole when the doorbell rang.

I flipped down a pair of Oakley wrap-around sunglasses and, still holding a pair of little Anthony's cotton briefs in one hand, opened the front door.

The light, still painfully bright, poured in from outside. I squinted behind my shades and could just made out the image of a UPS deliveryman.

And, oh, what an image it was.

As my eyes adjusted to the light, a hunky guy with tan legs and beefy arms materialized through the screen door before me. He grinned at me easily, showing off a perfect row of white teeth. Spiky yellow hair protruded from under his brown cap. The guy should have been a model, or at least my new best friend.

"Mrs. Moon?" he asked. His eyes seemed particularly searching and hungry, and I wondered if I had stepped onto the set of a porno movie. Interestingly, a sort of warning bell sounded in my head. Warning bells are tricky to discern, and I automatically assumed this one was telling me to stay away from Mr. Beefy, or risk damaging my already rocky marriage.

"You got her," I said easily, ignoring the warning bells.

"I've got a package here for you."

"You don't say."

"I'll need for you to sign the delivery log." He held up an electronic gizmo-thingy that must have been the aforementioned delivery log.

"I'm sure you do," I said, and opened the screen door and stuck a hand out. He looked at my very pale hand, paused, and then placed the electronic thing-a-majig in it. As I signed it, using a plastic-tipped pen, my signature appeared in the display box as an arthritic mess. The deliveryman watched me intently through the screen door. I don't like to be watched intently. In fact, I prefer to be ignored and forgotten.

"Do you always wear sunglasses indoors?" he asked casually, but I sensed his hidden question: *And what sort of freak are you?*

"Only during the day. I find them redundant at night." I opened the screen door again and exchanged the log doohickey for a small square package. "Thank you," I said. "Have a good day."

He nodded and left, and I watched his cute little buns for a moment longer, and then shut the solid oak door completely. Sweet darkness returned to my home. I pulled up the sunglasses and sat down in a particularly worn dining room chair. Someday I was going to get these things re-upholstered.

The package was heavily taped, but a few deft strokes of my painted red nail took care of all that. I opened the lid and peered inside. Shining inside was an ancient golden medallion. An intricate Celtic cross was engraved across the face of it, and embedded within the cross, formed by precisely cut rubies, were three red roses.

In the living room, Judge Judy was calmly explaining to the defendant what an idiot he was. Although I agreed, I turned the TV off, deciding that this medallion needed my full concentration.

After all, it was the same medallion worn by my attacker six years earlier.

CHAPTER TWO

There was no return address and no note. Other than the medallion, the box was empty. I left the gleaming artifact in the box and shut the lid. Seeing it again brought back some horrible memories. Memories I have been doing my best to forget.

I put the box in a cabinet beneath the china hutch, and then went back to Judge Judy and putting away the laundry. At 3:30 p.m., I lathered my skin with heaping amounts of sun block, donned a wide gardening hat and carefully stepped outside.

The pain, as always, was intense and searing. Hell, I could have been cooking over an open fire pit. Truly, I had no business being out in the sun, but I had my kids to pick up, dammit.

So I hurried from the front steps and crossed the driveway and into the open garage. My dream was to have a home with an attached garage. But, for now, I had to make the daily sprint.

Once in the garage and out of the direct glare of the spring sun, I could breathe again. I could also smell my burning flesh.

Blech!

Luckily, the Ford Windstar minivan was heavily tinted, and so when I backed up and put the thing into drive, I was doing okay again. Granted, not great, but okay.

I picked up my son and daughter from school, got some cheeseburgers from Burger King and headed home. Yes, I know, bad mom, but after doing chores all day, I definitely was *not* going to cook.

Once at home, the kids went straight to their room and I went straight to the bathroom where I removed my hat and sunglasses, and used a washcloth to remove the extra sunscreen. Hell, I ought to buy stock in Coppertone. Soon the kids were hard at work saving our world from Haloes and had lapsed into a rare and unsettling silence. Perhaps it was the quiet before the storm.

My only appointment for the day was right on time, and since I work from home, I showed him to my office in the back. His name was Kingsley Fulcrum and he sat across from me in a client chair, filling it to capacity. He was tall and broad shouldered and wore his tailored suit well. His thick black hair, speckled with gray, was jauntily disheveled and worn long over his collar. Kingsley was a striking man and would have been the poster boy for dashing rogues if not for the two scars on his face. Then again, maybe poster boys for rogue did have scars on their faces. Anyway, one was on his left cheek and the other was on his forehead, just above his left eye. Both were round and puffy. And both were recent.

He caught me staring at the scars. I looked away, embarrassed. "How can I help you, Mr. Fulcrum?"

"How long have you been a private investigator, Mrs. Moon?" he asked.

"Six years," I said.

"What did you do before that?"

"I was a federal agent."

He didn't say anything, and I could feel his eyes on me. God, I hate when I can feel eyes on me. The silence hung for longer than I was comfortable with and I answered his unspoken question. "I had an accident and was forced to work at home."

"May I ask what kind of accident?"

"No."

He raised his eyebrows and nodded. He might have turned a pale shade of red. "Do you have a list of references?"

"Of course."

I turned to my computer, brought up the reference file and printed him out the list. He took it and scanned the names briefly. "Mayor Hartley?" he asked.

"Yes," I said.

"He hired you?"

"He did. I believe that's the direct line to his personal assistant."

"Can I ask what sort of help you gave the mayor?"

"No."

"I understand. Of course you can't divulge that kind of information."

"How exactly can I help you, Mr. Fulcrum?" I asked again.

"I need you to find someone."

"Who?"

"The man who shot me," he said. "Five times."

CHAPTER THREE

The furious sounds of my kids erupting into an argument suddenly came through my closed office door. In particular, Anthony's high-pitched shriek. Sigh. The storm broke.

I gave Kingsley an embarrassed smile. "Could you please hold on?"

"Duty calls," he said, smiling. Nice smile.

I marched through my single story home and into the small bedroom my children shared. Anthony was on top of Tammy. Tammy was holding the remote control away from her body with one hand and fending off her little brother with the other. I came in just in time to witness him sinking his teeth into her hand. She yelped and bopped him over the ear with the remote control. He had just gathered himself to make a full-scale leap onto her back, when I stepped into the room and grabbed each by their collar and separated them. I felt as if I had separated two ravenous wolverines. Anthony's fingers clawed for his sister's throat. I wondered if they realized they were both hovering a few inches off the floor. When they had both calmed down, I set them down on their feet. Their collars were ruined.

"Anthony, we do not bite in this household. Tammy, give me the remote control."

"But Mom," said Anthony, in that shriekingly high-pitched voice that he used to irritate me. "I was watching 'Pokemon' and she turned the channel."

"We each get one half hour after school," Tammy said smugly. "And you were well into *my* half hour."

"But you were on the phone talking to *Richaaard.*"

"Tammy, give your brother the remote control. He gets to finish his TV show. You lost your dibs by talking to *Richaaard.*" They both laughed. "I have a client in my office. If I hear any more loud voices, you will both be auctioned off on eBay. I could use the extra money."

I left them and headed back to the office. Kingsley was perusing my bookshelves. He looked at me before I had a chance to say anything and raised his eyebrows.

"You have an interest in the occult," he said, fingering a hardback book. "In particular, vampirism."

"Yeah, well, we all need a hobby," I said.

"An interesting hobby, that," he said.

I sat behind my desk. It was time to change the subject. "So you want me to find the man who shot you five times. Anything else?"

He moved away from my book shelves and sat across from me again. He raised a fairly bushy eyebrow. On him, the bushy eyebrow somehow worked.

"Anything else?" he asked, grinning. "No, I think that will be quite enough."

And then it hit me. I *thought* I recognized the name and face. "You were on the news a few months back," I said suddenly.

He nodded once. "Aye, that was me. Shot five times in the head for all the world to see. Not my proudest moment."

Did he just say *aye*? I had a strange sense that I had suddenly gone back in time. How far back, I didn't know, but further enough back where men said *aye*.

"You were ambushed and shot. I can't imagine it would have been anyone's proudest moment. But you survived, and that's all that matters, right?"

"For now," he said. "Next on the list would be to find the man who shot me." He sat forward. "Everything you need is at your disposal. Nothing of mine is off limits. Speak to anyone you need to, although I ask you to be discreet."

"Discretion is sometimes not possible."

"Then I trust you to use your best judgment."

Good answer. He took out a business card and wrote something on the back. "That's my cell number. Please call me if you need anything." He wrote something under his number. "And that's the name and number of the acting homicide detective working my case. His name is Sherbet, and although I found him to be forthcoming and professional, I didn't like his conclusions."

"Which were?"

"He tends to think my attack was nothing but a random shooting."

"And you disagree?"

"Wholeheartedly."

We discussed my retainer and he wrote me a check. The check was bigger than we discussed.

"I don't mean to be rude," said Kingsley as he stood and tucked his expensive fountain pen inside his expensive jacket, "but are you ill?"

I've heard the question a thousand times.

"No, why?" I asked brightly.

"You seem pale."

"Oh, that's my Irish complexion, lad," I said, and winked.

He stared at me a moment longer, and then returned my wink and left.

ABOUT THE AUTHORS

Piers Anthony is one of the world's most prolific and popular authors. His fantasy Xanth novels have been read and loved by millions of readers around the world, and have been on the New York Times Best Seller list twenty-one times. Although Piers is mostly known for fantasy and science fiction, he has written several novels in other genres as well, including historical fiction, martial arts, and horror. Piers lives with his wife in a secluded woods hidden deep in Central Florida.

Please visit him at www.hipiers.com for a complete list of his fiction and non-fiction and to read his monthly newsletter.

J.R. Rain is an ex-private investigator who now writes full-time. He lives in a small house on a small island with his small dog, Sadie, who has more energy than Robin Williams.

Please visit him at www.jrrain.com.

Made in the USA
Charleston, SC
06 September 2014